ORIGINAL SERIES

Silver PLATTER HOE 3

SHIT JUST GOT REAL...

REDS JOHNSON

Silver Platter Hoe 3:
Shit Just Got Real

*This book as well as many more is dedicated to my ridah. My beautiful mother **Maria Ward**. We were homeless together so we gon' eat together. I love you beyond life itself lady.*

*R*obert sat at his computer dumbfounded he couldn't believe the email he just saw. He never would have thought in a million years that his partner would do the things that he did.

"What's wrong Robert?" Mattie asked in a worried tone. She could see Robert's facial expression from the computer and she could tell it wasn't good.

"THAT BASTARD!" Robert yelled as he pounded his fist on the table.

Mattie jumped "Robert what's wrong?" she asked again.

"I've been trying to see if anyone had any leads on who could possibly do this to Desire, and I just got an email from the captain. He's been calling me telling me that he had some news he wanted to share with me, but I've been so busy so I told him he should just email me. Detective Johnson has been the one letting out Desire and Rell's information that's how Diane and Terrence knew where they lived," Robert told her.

"Oh, Lord why would he do that?" she asked.

"I don't know, but I have to let Desire and Rell know this is serious," he told her.

Mattie picked up her bible. "Lord I ask that you help us rebuke the devil I ask in the name of Jesus."

"Mattie ain't nobody got time for that right now," Robert said cutting her off.

He printed out the email and shut down his computer. He grabbed his coat and car keys and headed out the door. Robert wasted no time dipping and dodging out of traffic to get to Desire and Rell's house. He got there in no time, after hopping out of the car he ran to the door and banged on it. After about 5 minutes of banging on the door it slung open and Rell stood there wrapped in a towel with soap dripping from his body

"Da fuck wrong witchu bruh?" he asked with a scowl on his face.

"We have to talk, this is important," Robert told him.

"About what?" Rell asked.

"Me and my captain go way back so whatever he finds out that concerns me he lets me know. He sent me an email, here it is," Robert said as he handed it to Rell.

He unfolded the paper and started reading. Robert could tell by Rell's flared nostrils that he wasn't happy about what he just read.

"I can see you're just as angry as I am," Robert stated.

Rell shook his head in disbelief. "So, after all the bullshit me and Desire been through we been getting played like a fiddle this whole time" Rell said.

"I believe we've all been played. Detective Johnson is the one who has been giving out you and Desire's information that's how Diane and Terrence knew where you all lived, but there's something else you should read," Robert said as he handed Rell the other folded paper.

Rell opened it and couldn't believe what he saw it was the results of the DNA that they found underneath desires nails.

"Terrence didn't try to kill desire it was Detective Johnson!" Rell said. Robert shook his head yes.

"**S**o, you sure she's dead?" Trina asked.

"Yea even though that little bitch scratched me I gutted her like a fish, and to prove it I brought you both a little present," Donnie said as he pulled out a little plastic baggy that contained blood and flesh.

"What the fuck is that?" Terrence asked as he jumped back.

"Trina's niece or nephew," he told them. Trina smiled from ear to ear. "Damn dad, well done," Trina said.

Donnie sat down and lit up a cigar. "You see back in my day that little bitch would have been shot execution style but I did her a favor." he said as he took a pull of his cigar.

"My question is how did you even get that close to her without Rell biting your head off," Trina asked.

"She gotta point there," Terrence agreed. "I'm not a newbie to putting in work now. So, don't think for one second that the shit I pulled off is something that I've never done before." Donnie told them.

"I'm not saying that. I'm just asking a question," Trina said.

"I left for North Carolina the day before. I was actually just supposed to watch their every move, but after yawl called me and told me the little show she put on my plans changed and I waited until they got back home and that's when I made my move," he told them.

"So, my bro wasn't anywhere to be found?" asked Terrence.

"He dropped her off home and went about his merry little way," said Donnie.

"Well, if you ask me I'm glad she's dead. I don't care how it happened but I'm glad that bitch is history!" Trina said as she took stacks of money out of her purse.

"Where the fuck did you get all that?" Terrence asked. "I never kiss and tell," Trina responded.

Terrence just shook his head because he already knew how she got the money. "Yo, I swear if I catch something I'ma kill you!" Terrence told her.

"Boy bye ain't nobody thinking about you!" Trina said.

"Iight keep on witcha bullshit," said Terrence.

"So, what do we do now?" Trina asked.

"We kill Terrell next and that faggot son of his," said Donnie.

"Well, all of us gotta go at Terrell together because he's not going down without a fight," Trina told them.

*R*ell sat in his new mini condo thinking about everything that had went on in such little time. He was forced to find another place after desire was almost killed in their other home.

"Damn, why would he want to do something like this to Des?" mark asked.

"That's the thing I don't know. I've been searching for answers since I found out that he did it, but I keep coming up with nothing," said Robert.

Rell sat quietly he was letting everything soak in which was all too much for him.

"Well I'ma def see what I can find out," Mark told him.

"What can you possibly find out?" Robert asked.

"Watchu think just because you a Detective that you know everything? Fuck outta here man I'm from the streets and the streets talk. So, like I said I'MA SEE WHAT I CAN FIND OUT!" Mark stated.

Robert said nothing. He knew he had just put his foot in his mouth so he had no come back.

"Are you going to be ok?" Robert asked.

"Yea I'ma be good Desire is a strong girl. She will be back in no time," Rell said.

"Ok, well I guess Mark and I will get back to you in a few days when we find out something. Oh, and I think that we should put this in the newspaper," said Robert.

"Da fuck for?" Mark barked.

"Someone tried to kill Desire so to keep her safe we should put that she was killed in the newspaper," said Robert.

This whole situation didn't sit right with Rell. He didn't like the things that Robert was suggesting

"Look do what you wanna do." Rell said.

Mark looked at Robert then to Rell "Some shit just ain't what it seems ma 'G."

Mark told Rell as he gave him dap. Mark was speaking in code so Rell was already hip to it. After they were gone Rell called his mother

"What you doing?" he asked once she answered.

"Nothing, where's my TJ?" she asked.

"He's sleeping you feel like going for a ride?" he asked.

"Where to?", "Just be ready in 15 minutes" Rell told her ignoring her question.

"A woman like me can never get ready in 15 minutes," Debra told him.

"Oh, please cut it out be ready in 15 minutes or get left," he said and ended the call.

Rell went into TJ's room and woke him up "Come on little man we going bye byes." Rell told him.

"We go see Mommy?" TJ asked.

"No, Mommy will be home in a few days," Rell told him.

He got TJ dressed and then put on his coat "Daddy I want ice cream," said TJ.

"Ok, daddy will get you ice cream later," Rell told him.

He grabbed TJ's diaper bag and made sure everything was locked up. Rell put TJ in his car seat and buckled him in. Afterwards he got in the car and pulled off. It's been a week since Desire was hurt and she was still in a coma and Rell didn't know how much more he could take. His Aunt told him to keep praying and that everything would be fine but for once Rell wasn't so sure. He pulled up to his mother house and beeped. 10 minutes passed and she still didn't come out so he called her phone

"I thought I said be ready in 15?" Rell said.

"And I thought I told you that I can't be ready in 15 minutes," Debra shot back.

"Well your about to get left," Rell told her.

"Oh, hush up I'm grabbing my jacket now," she told him and hung up.

Rell watched as his mother came out and locked the doors. She trotted to the car and got in.

"You do realize that your 45, right?" Rell asked.

"And exactly what is that supposed to mean?" asked Debra.

"Stop dressing like you young," Rell told her.

"Rell please, just because I dress nice doesn't mean I dress young. Hell, I look good to be 45 now Shut yo ass up tryna insult me!" Debra said.

Rell laughed and kept driving "Terrell where are we going?" Debra asked.

"Ring shopping," he said finally.

"OH, MY GOSH YOUR GONNA PROPOSE TO DESIRE?" she squealed.

Terrell laughed. "Yes, Mom I'm going to propose to Desire on our 4year anniversary hopefully she's out of the coma by then." Rell said.

"Terrell sweetie she is in a temporary coma she will be back don't worry," Debra said.

"Yea but we might have another setback," Rell told her.

Debra looked over at him. "What do you mean?" she asked.

"Detective Johnson is the reason why Desire is in the hospital," Rell told her.

"Isn't that Desire's Uncle's partner?" she asked.

"Yea their no longer partners though," Rell said

"Well why would he do such a thing like that?" Debra asked.

"I don't know that's what we all tryna figure out now," Rell said as he pulled into the mall parking lot. Rell got out and got TJ out of his car seat.

"My precious grandson," Debra said as she took him from Rell.

"You spoil him too much!" Rell told her.

"Oh, please, he just reminds me so much of you when you were a kid. I'm just so thankful to have a grandchild, and our family so damn crazy I wanna spend as much time with him as possible." Debra said.

They entered Zale's and Debra instantly fell in love.

"Terrell, do you see this?" she said in excitement.

"Yea this one is nice as hell," he said.

"Hello how can I help you all today?" said one of the men behind the counters.

"Hi, we would like to see your engagement rings," Debra asked.

"Ok, well over here we have some of our best. This is actually my favorite because its white gold," he told them.

"This is it, this is the one," Rell said.

"Are you sure? You didn't even look at the rest," Debra said.

"This caught my eye I don't need to look at the rest I want that one," he told her.

"Well that's an excellent choice that is our Certified Radiant-Cut Diamond Bridal Set in 24K White Gold," he said as he took it out and handed it to Rell.

"That is beautiful," Debra said.

"How much is it?" Rell asked.

"Well we do have a payment plan because I'm sure you can't afford to pay it in full right now," he told them.

Rell looked at the man. "I didn't ask for your judgmental ass comments now how much is it?" Rell asked again.

The man rung everything up before he spoke "Your total is $5,339.00. Will that be cash or credit?" he asked.

"Credit," Rell said and took out his black card and the man's eyes lit up.

He swiped it and signed the receipt "Well thank you for shopping with us today you have a good after noon," the man told them.

"Yea, whatever and next time don't judge a book by its cover. Just because I'm black doesn't mean I'm broke," Rell said and grabbed his bag, but before he could walk out TJ called him "Daddy look!" he said as he pointed at the jewelry. Rell walked over and seen that TJ was pointing at the same exact chain that he had on his neck

"I want this Daddy," TJ told him.

"I swear if this isn't ya twin," Debra said.

Rell smiled. "Yo smart ass, give me this chain right here," Rell told him.

"This is $1,300.00 sir," said the man.

"Damn nigga, I know the price now either you shut the fuck up talking to me or I'ma light this store up like the 4th of July," Rell warned.

"Yes, yes sir, I'm getting your things together right now," the man said quickly.

Rell picked up TJ and sat him on the counter.

"Don't even wrap it up just give it to me," Rell said.

He gave Rell the chain and Rell put it on TJ's neck. "Like Father Like Son," Rell said as he got TJ down and grabbed his bags and walked out.

"I can't believe you are married I raised you right and I am proud of myself," Debra told him.

"Yea, I feel like it's time. She's been down for me since day one/ I love that girl with all my heart and I don't wanna be with nobody else but her," he told her.

"I'm proud of you. I really am and I don't want you nor Desire to worry about what that doctor said about her not being able to have kids again because the lord has the last say you hear me," Debra said.

"Yea mom I hear you. I don't know how I'ma tell her this once she comes back," Rell told her.

"Well, we will cross that bridge when the time comes. Now let's go see if she's made any progress," she told him.

"YEA, FUCK THIS ASS, FUCK IT!" Trina screamed as Terrence pounded away. Donnie sat in the corner and watched as he rubbed his dick.

"You like when I tear yo ass up don't you?" Terrence asked as he yanked on her 22' inch pony tail.

"Yea Daddy I like it when you make it hurt!" Trina moaned.

Terrence pulled out and laid back on the bed.

"Suck it," he said as he pushed her head down.

Trina licked the tip of his dick and then swallowed him whole. Donnie got up and stripped down to his boxers, Trina looked up and smiled

"I guess you couldn't help yourself, you liked what you saw," she said.

Trina could see from the bulge that he was packing something serious. Donnie walked over to Trina as she was jerking off Terrence. He pulled down his boxers and Trina's guess was right he was packing something serious his 12 ½ chocolate dick hung loosely between his legs. Trina climbed on top of Terrence and started to ride him like never before. She wanted to put on a good show for Donnie and it was working because his monster stood at attention. He climbed on the bed and got behind Trina. He spit on the tip of his fingers and then rubbed them on the head of his dick before he slid it in. Trina gasped as he entered her.

"Yea you feel that dick filling up that asshole," Donnie grunted as he moved in and out of her slowly.

"Yea daddy I feel it and it feels so damn good," she moaned.

For the next 2 hours Donnie and Terrence had sexed Trina in all three holes. They treated her like the whore she was and the sad part about it was that she loved every bit of it.

"Here," said Terrence as he threw 2 stacks at her

"What is this you said I was getting $3,500.00," Trina said with attitude

"No, he said that I told you I was giving you what I had on me so don't trip. Ain't nobody tell you to fuck both of us bitch," Terrence barked.

"Now, now settle down you will get your money when I go to the bank in the morning. I don't carry that kind of money on me, and you know that," said Donnie.

Trina rolled her eyes and snatched up her money. "Niggas ain't shit!" she said and then stormed in the bathroom.

"Yea but that ain't never stopped you from fucking and sucking us," Terrence yelled back. Donnie laughed and sat down on the couch. He pulled out a cigar and lit it up.

"I see we have a lot in common son," said Donnie.

Terrence sat back on the bed and flicked on the TV "How so?" he asked.

"Well I know a little bit about you and I see that we do some of the same things," he told him.

"Yea like what?" Terrence asked uninterested.

"Well, let's just say we like to keep it in the family," said Donnie with a laugh.

*T*errell was on his way to get him and TJ some food
when his phone rung.

"Hello," he answered.

"Terrell she's a wake baby. SHE'S AWAKE! THANK
YOU, JESUS!" his mom screamed into the phone. His heart
dropped he couldn't believe it after almost a month Desire
was finally back.

"I'll be there, ok?" he told her.

"Ok, baby I'll see you there," she said and ended the call.

He didn't express his feelings on the phone but Rell was
filled with joy. He couldn't wait to see her. He needed to hear
her voice. After getting him and TJ's food, he wasted no time
getting to the hospital.

He found a close parking spot and got out "I got a surprise for you little man." Rell said as he held TJ's hand and carried their food in the other hand.

"What?" TJ asked

"Just wait and see, but first we gotta go in this store right here and get a few gifts," Rell said he bought Desire flowers and balloons and he let TJ pick out a card and bought a pen to write with. They made their way to her room.

"Wait, Daddy gotta write on this card real quick," Rell said, so they stayed outside until he was finished. After about 5 minutes he was done Rell and TJ walked into the room and saw Desire sitting up.

"MOMMY!" TJ screamed as he ran to her bedside.

Desire smiled weakly, she had to stare at him for a minute because she couldn't quite remember certain things, but once TJ got into her arms and his scent hit her nose she knew exactly who he was

"Hey baby," she said.

Her voice was scratchy and dry. Robert and Mattie and his mother sat around her as Rell got closer Desire looked up and smiled at him. She still had minor bruises but she was still the most beautiful girl in the world to him.

"Hey babe this is for you," Terrell said as he handed her the flowers and card. He put the balloons beside her.

"Thank you," Desire said. Rell noticed that Desire didn't bother to open the card.

"Rell let me talk to you in private," Debra said. They went outside the room

"Desire doesn't remember much. The doctor said it was normal and as each day passes she will start to remember more and more. However, Robert has been saying some things that I don't like," Debra told him.

Rell looked down at the ground "This is all my fault if I was there none of this would've happened and what has he been saying?" he asked.

"This is not your fault baby and Desire is fine she may not be able to remember certain things but at least she is still alive and he doesn't want her to mention this to anyone. He's basically telling her to brush it off," Debra said.

Rell didn't want to talk anymore he just wanted to be around Desire. He had a funny feeling about a lot of stuff, but he wanted Desire to be 100 % better before he brought anything to her attention. He walked back into the room and pulled a chair up beside her.

"Can we be alone please?" Rell said.

"Remember what I told you?" Robert said to Desire before leaving.

"So how you feeling?" he asked.

"I'm sore and my head feels cloudy but I'm ok," she told him.

"Do you remember who I am?" he asked. Desire looked at him,

"Yes, I do," She told him

"Who am I?" Rell asked her.

"My boyfriend silly just because I was in a coma doesn't mean I couldn't hear you."

Desire said as she cleared her throat. Rell smiled.

"So, you knew that I was here with you?" he asked.

"Yes, I did," she told him.

"Well can you read the card I brought you?" he said as he handed it to her.

Desire opened the card and read it.

"Desire, I know this last year or so haven't been the best for us, but I want you to know I love you dearly. When I first met you, it was love at first sight. I loved everything about you from your smile all the way down to your walk. When you told me, you was pregnant with my first child I was lifted with joy. The little family we have created warms my heart every day. I want you to know that you're my first love. No other woman in this world will ever take the spot you have in my heart; you and TJ are my everything. I'm not risking that for nothing or nobody. My loyalty and love is all with you and TJ. I never want you

to forget that. You are my queen and TJ is my prince I want this forever, Love Rell."

Desire smiled at the card she may not have remember how she got in the hospital but she remembered her family.

6

"You think she gone find out?" Briana said as she put her clothes back on.

"Fuck her Trina and I ain't together," said Terrence.

"I just don't want her to get mad, since you and I are sleeping around," Briana said.

"I don't give a fuck if she finds out or not. I'm 30 years old I'll be 31 in 5 days and I stick my dick in any pussy I want!" Terrence told her.

Briana smiled and laid on his chest.

"I love you," she told him.

Terrence pushed her off him.

"Bitch love don't live here if you want love then you better get ya shit and go find it!" Terrence snapped.

"Seriously so what was all that shit you were saying when we were fuckin?" Briana spat.

"BITCH PILLOW TALK!" Terrence yelled.

"You so damn dumb that happens after sex that's why it's called pillow talk because we lay on the pillow and talk to each other," Briana said.

Terrence glanced at her and got up and started putting on his clothes

"Yea bitch I'm out," he told her.

"Wait baby don't go," she begged.

"Nah, get off me I'm out," he told her.

"What can I do to get you to stay?" she pleaded.

"Look get you a high school diploma and then maybe we can talk, but until then don't ever, ever, ever, ever, ever, ever call me again ok?" said Terrence and then he walked out.

As he was walking to his car he seen a Silver Lincoln Navigator the windows were tinted so he couldn't make out who it was. He got in his car and started it and the Navigator did the same. Terrence waited to see if they were going to pull off first but they didn't, so he waited. After about 10 minutes he finally pulled off and the Navigator followed. 25 minutes later Terrence finally reached his destination Pine hill, NJ. The Navigator stopped, did a U- turn and parked on the other side of the road. No one got out, so he thought. Terrence got out of his car and took his gun out.

He slowly crept up to the driver's side of the truck and slung the door open. To his surprise the truck was empty.

"The fuck is going on?" Terrence said.

Without notice, he felt cold steel touching his temple.

"Back up slowly muthafucka," the voice said. Terrence did as he was told but kept a tight grip on his .45.

"Turn around," The man told him.

Terrence slowly turned around.

"MAN GET THE FUCK OUTTA HERE!" Terrence yelled in disbelief.

"You always were an ignorant muthafucka well now the tables done turned, and its ma time to pay you back for all the bullshit you did to me," he said.

He took the butt of his gun and hit Terrence right in the head with it.

*D*esire was having a semi great recovery. She still couldn't do all that she wanted. Eat like she wanted but she was thankful to be alive.

"Good afternoon bae," Desire said when she walked in the kitchen.

Rell smiled.

"Good afternoon I guess somebody was up all night," he said sarcastically.

Desire rolled her eyes and got a cup of orange juice. She went over and wrapped her arms around Rell's neck while he was sitting, looking on the computer.

"Well that's because you kept me up all night and I enjoyed every bit of that love making," she told him.

He looked back and gave her a kiss.

"What you doing?" Des asked.

"Nothing," Rell said as he quickly shut the laptop.

Desire gave him a strange look because she knew he was up to something.

"Is TJ taking a nap or just sleeping late?" Des asked.

"No, he's taking a nap I gave him some Tylenol because he had a slight fever," Rell said.

"Yea I hate when he's sick he looks so sad. You know what the bad part about everything is?" Desire said.

"What's that?" he asked.

"I didn't even remember how old TJ was. I mean I knew he was my son but the basic things I didn't remember. The doctor said that it was all normal and he said as time goes on my memory will be back to normal," she told him.

"Yea I was a little concerned about that too, but I talked to your doctor as well and I feel confident in your recovery now," Rell told her.

"Well I'm glad because I want your birthday to be special," Desire said.

"Well to be honest my birthday is going to be special because I got you and TJ in my life. I still got time to handle mines and I'm tryna fuck some shit up," Rell told her.

"What do you mean?" Des asked.

"Just know I got somebody handling Terrence and I'ma handle that bitch ass Detective Johnson," Rell told her.

"Well I want in on this Rell! I'm serious I want this bitch ass nigga just as much as you do!" Des told him.

"I know Des, but at least heal up some more. I got a lot more shit I need to find out before anything jumps off," Rell said.

"A lot more stuff like what?" she asked. Rell looked at her.

"Some shit just ain't sittin' right with a nigga," he told her.

"Well if it's concerning me then I deserve to know," Desire said.

"I feel you bae all this shit got me thinking like why us. I mean first it was Trina now its Terrence and then now Detective Johnson," Rell said changing the subject.

"Speaking of Detective Johnson how did yawl find out it was him who did this to me?" Des asked.

"You scratched him and his skin and blood was under your nails. That wasn't nothing but God because the only thing they had was a foot print in the blood that was on the floor," Rell told her.

"I can't believe it I mean I barely remember anything that happened that day and my uncle keeps saying that's a good thing," Desire said.

"Don't worry bae it will all come back to you and yea did you see the newspaper article?" Rell told her.

"About me being dead yea, I saw it, but the story is a crock of bullshit," Desire said.

"That's exactly what I said when I read it," Rell told her. Desire touched her stomach and winced a little bit because it was still very sensitive and the staples were still there.

"Did they find my baby?" she asked.

Rell looked at her but didn't answer

"Rell answer me!" Desire said.

"No Des they didn't but I don't wanna talk about that right now," he told her.

"Rell we have to. I mean do you realize that I can no longer have kids," she told him.

Rell ignored Desire. He didn't want to talk about that because it was a touchy subject for him and the more he thought about it the more he became emotional and now wasn't the time for that.

*I*t was a day before Rell's birthday and desire wanted everything to be perfect. She ordered him a cake with a strawberry cheesecake filling and gave Debra money and the list of gifts she wanted to get him.

"Mark, you better not take him nowhere crazy," Des told them.

"I'm not, just chill we ain't off that," Mark told her.

"I hear you, but don't keep him out too long. I'm tryna bring his birthday in right while TJ is spending the night at his grandma's," Des told him.

"Too much information yo Rell hurry up slime Des out here talking nasty," Mark yelled to him.

Desire laughed at Mark and almost melted at the sight of Rell. He came out in a white tee with some dark blue denim jeans and his cream timberlands with a fitted hat to match as his braids hung loosely down his back.

"You out here scaring ma boy away Des?" Rell asked.

"Ain't nobody scaring Mark away, and you lookin' tasty as ever." Des told him.

"Thanks bae and I'll be back in a few hours," Rell told her.

Desire pulled him close and her tongue met his. Mark looked on in awe as they kissed like that was their first time.

"Ok now go have fun," Desire told him.

"I love you."

"I love you too," Desire said.

Rell and Mark headed to his car.

"Damn man yawl been together for almost 4 years and yawl still act like it's the first-time yawl met," Mark told him.

"Man, I love that girl. I got something special for her on our anniversary," Rell said.

"Yea what's that?" Mark asked.

"I'ma propose to her," he said.

"WHAT! Aw shit ma nigga getting married I'm the best man, right?" Mark asked.

Rell laughed "Man hell yea you already know that!" Rell told him.

"I betta be its crazy how I known you since I was 13, and I never would've thought that you would get a girl like Desire. No disrespect, but we was some hoes and it seemed like that's all we attracted at the time," said Mark.

"Yea you right, but I'm thankful that I got a woman like her. I mean we go through our bullshit but that's my heart; her and TJ and I'm just ready for us to get rid of all the bullshit in our lives. I'm tired of killin' niggas," Rell said and they both bust out laughing.

They went to the strip club to have a few drinks but Rell really wasn't feeling the scenery. He had a woman at home so he wasn't entertained at all and the niggas was paying more attention to him than the strippers.

"Damn, I can't go nowhere without a nigga hatin'," Rell said as he got up to leave.

"These fuck niggas don't want no problems," Mark said as he pulled his shirt up showing his .45.

The dudes quickly backed down and turned their heads but one of them wanted to get buff.

"Yo, what set you bangin'?" said a tall skinny dude that had the skin color of charcoal.

Rell stopped in his tracks he couldn't believe niggas was still gangbanging.

"Man, fuck outta ma face with that shit!" Rell barked.

The guy tried to get in Rell's face but Mark slid in between them with his gun drawn.

"Oh, we gotta problem? Shit, because if we do then I don't mind putting a nigga head on a platter tonight," said Mark.

"Nah, we cool man I just thought yawl was some lil niggas out here false flagging that's all ma G," the guy pleaded.

"Yea, I thought you might switch up we cool dog?" Mark asked Rell.

Rell gave the dude a quick smirk.

"Yea man these niggas ain't bout that action we cool," he told him.

"Iight muthafucka, I'ma give you a pass but next time it's off wit' ya muthafuckin' head. Now go over there with ya homies and enjoy the rest of ya night," Mark told the guy and shooed him away.

They left out and got into the car.

"It must be ma baby face cuz these niggas be trying me like I'ma young boy or some shit," Rell said.

"Yea you do look young as shit," Mark said with a laugh.

"Shut the fuck up," Rell said playfully.

"Yo, but on a real note that nigga Robert been rubbing me the wrong way," said Mark.

"Yea bro I feel you some shit just don't sit well with me either, but check this I looked this nigga up and guess what," Rell said.

"What's that?" Mark replied.

"This nigga not even a detective," Rell said.

Mark looked at him, but you can tell he wasn't surprised at all because he already felt a certain kind of way towards Robert when he first met him.

"I knew it was something fishy about this nigga," Mark said as he shook his head.

They hit the mall to do a little shopping, but ended up spending more than they planned.

"Yo, Des gone be pissed that I spent almost 3 stacks in the mall on nothing," Rell said.

"Man, this shit adds up though," Mark told him.

"Yea it do, but I'm hungry let's go to Apple Bee's," Rell said.

"Iight cool," Mark responded.

They headed to Apple Bees and went ham.

"Yo, they be takin mad long but the food is good as hell," Rell said.

"Man, I can't wait until Thanksgiving I know Des gone throw down," Mark said.

"You know she is," Rell responded.

"It always is real busy this time of the year because of yawl birthdays and the holidays but I ain't complaining because it's always food and cake involved," said Mark

Rell just shook his head at Mark. He was a funny nigga he been down with Rell since day one. They got into a lot of shit together and they were always loyal to one another they were more like brothers than friends.

"It's going on 9 already we might as well just go back to the house and play the game until I get ready to break Des back," Rell said.

"Yawl nasty. She gone pop up pregnant again watch man fuck what that doctor said," Mark stated.

Rell got quiet. He really didn't like talking about that because it was a sensitive subject for him.

"Ma bad bro I ain't mean to bother you by bringing that up," Mark told him.

"Nah man you good shit happens," Rell said trying to play it cool.

The ride home was silent, but both Mark and Rell was lost in their thoughts about everything that's been happening. They made it back to the house by 10:00. When they Rell and Mark entered the house the smell of sweet vanilla filled the air. There was soft music playing and the lights were dim.

"Damn man should I even be here?" Mark asked.

Before Rell could answer desire came down the hall in a skin tight sheer black dress that looked like it was painted on.

"You ready for your early birthday present daddy?" Desire said

She stopped in her tracks when she saw Mark.

"RELL!" She yelled as she ran back down the hallway.

They both bust out laughing.

"Yo, I'ma dip out back to the hotel Ima catch you tomorrow man enjoy yaself," Mark said.

"Ight ma dude," Rell said as he gave him dap.

Mark left out and Rell took off his jacket. Desire came back down the hallway.

"I was hoping to surprise you. I didn't know Mark was coming in," she told him.

Rell walked over and grabbed desire around the waist.

"Baby girl I'm very surprised and yes I'm ready for my early birthday present," he said as he stuck his tongue out.

Desire stuck hers out and twirled it around his. She pulled away and got down on her knees.

"Nah get up," he told her.

Rell never liked when Desire got on her knees to give him head it seemed way to degrading to him. She sat on the couch and unbuckled his pants. He was throbbing as she tugged to get his pants down. His thick dick plopped out once he was released.

"Mmmmm, he's happy to see mommy," Desire said and swallowed him whole.

Rell hissed as she swallowed him then spit him back out like a lollipop. She bobbed her head back and forth wildly. Rell grabbed her head to take control so he wouldn't nut too fast. He looked down, and Desire and he were giving each other direct eye contact. He stopped her and pulled her up. He kissed her hungrily. He picked her up and carried her to the bedroom. The room was lit up by vanilla scented candles. He laid desire on the bed and lifted he dress up. He wasn't surprised that she didn't have on any panties. He kissed between her thighs and gave her clit a peck which was peeking out between her lips. He tried to pull the dress up further but Desire stopped him. Since the incident every time him and Desire was intimate she would have a shirt on.

"Baby stop," Rell told her.

"Rell I can't it is bad enough I was insecure about my weight and now I have to worry about this damn scar," Desire said.

"Desire look at me," Rell told her. She looked up at him with teary eyes.

"Baby I love you. I've been telling you this for years. I'm happy with you and every part of you. I don't give a damn who don't like it I ain't going nowhere and I don't like when you get this way. You're my queen and queens don't lack in confidence now I got about an hour before my birthday and I'm tryna be digging in your guts when it comes," Rell told her.

Desire smiled and pulled her dress off. She loved the way Rell made her feel. He never judged her no matter how embarrassed she felt at times. He always made her feel special even though he was a hood nigga. She guided Rell's head down to her love cave and he dove in without a problem. Desire squirted, and Rell sucked her dry. Her clit was throbbing but he didn't care he got undress and enter her slowly. He moaned as he slipped inside her wetness. Rell gave her slow and deep strokes and she loved every bit of it. He picked up the pace and she bit her bottom lip as their bodies smacked together.

"Oooooooo! ooooh God Rell!" Desire gasped with each stroke Rell took.

"You love me Des?" Rell asked.

"Ye...Yes!!" Desire screamed.

"Are you gone give me another child?" Rell asked as he plugged deeper insider her.

"Rell! the... the...doctor said... I couldn't have kids!" she gasped.

"Fuck what the doctor said," Rell told her.

Des held on to him tight as he went deeper and deeper.

"Like I said, are you gone give me another child?" Rell asked again.

Desire thought about everything they had been through between Trina kidnapping TJ and Terrence being after Rell. She thought about Rell's real mom and what she took him through. She thought about her uncle being shot. She thought about what Terrence had done to her. She wanted her family to not only be safe but to be happy and if Rell wanted another child then she was going to give him one because life was way too short.

"Yes, I'll give you another child!" she told him and that was all he needed to hear as he released his seed inside her.

*R*ell's birthday had been a success he brought it in how he wanted and spent it with his family like he wanted. Everyone was so eager for the month, November to roll around. Not only was thanksgiving coming up but also Debra's birthday. Rell wanted his mother's birthday to be special so he told her to pick anywhere around the world that she wanted to go and he would pay. She decided that she wanted to go to Orlando, Florida and Rell made sure that happened.

"Hey babe," Rell said when Desire came in from grocery shopping.

"Hey honey bunch," Desire said as she walked over and kissed him.

"Wassup Des" Mark greeted.

"Hey bro pause the game and you and Rell go out and get those bags," Des said after hugging him.

They both blew loudly.

"Ummm, unless yawl wanna eat on thanksgiving I suggest yawl cut the bullshit and go get those bags," Des told them.

They both jumped up and headed outside. Desire shook her head. She loved them both Rell was her man and mark was the big brother she never had. Mark was staying with them for the holidays and he was considering getting a place there. Desire didn't mind at all she was glad he was around and not the rest of his boys from Jersey. They came back in with the bags and put them in the kitchen.

"Thank you," she said to them.

"Yea... Yea," Mark said and went back to sit down.

"I can see that you gone be cooking a lot for thanksgiving from the look of things," Rell said.

"Yup when your mother gets back from her mini vacation me, her and Mattie gone throw down," Des told him.

"Well you know I can't wait. I like to eat," Rell said

"Me too," Mark chimed in.

"I hope you know ya so called boys back in jersey is not invited," Des told Rell.

"I know Des," Rell said.

He pulled her towards him and kissed her.

"You are so stubborn you know, that right?" Rell said.

"No, I'm not I just know bullshit when I see it and your boys are bullshit the only loyal one is Mark," Desire said.

"Come on Des don't be like that," Rell told her.

Desire pushed him,

"Excuse me Rell, I am so tired of you protecting them weak ass niggas of yours! Since we been together I never liked them and they never liked me, but for some reason it's always Des chill! YOU NEVER SAY SHIT TO THOSE FUCK NIGGAS!" Des snapped.

"So, what you want me to do Des?" Rell asked.

Desire cocked her head to the side and looked at Rell like he was crazy.

"What the fuck do you mean what I want you to do your 31 years old you ain't stupid!" Des told him.

"Desire they ma boys I knew them since I was a youngin' like come on ma," Rell said.

"Oh, so I haven't been there I haven't been holding you down? What am I just some fuck toy? I mean really what's the problem? You keep saying they ya boys, but look what Amir did he set you up. LOOK AT WHAT KEVIN BITCH ASS DID BUT YOU WANNA SAY HE YA BOY TOO!" she yelled.

"I'm not about to sit here and argue with you over this. I'm really not Des because this shit doesn't need to be like this," Rell told her.

Desire was so fed up with everything she went to the bedroom and pulled her duffle bag out of the closet she put a couple of outfits in and went to TJ's room. She packed him some outfits and zipped up her bag. She went back into the living room

"Since it's all about yawl. Mark, you cook, clean, suck his dick and fuck him when he needs to be fucked. I'm done!" she yelled and grabbed her keys and stormed out. She left Rell and Mark both in complete shock.

"What the fuck just happened?" Rell asked in shock.

"Look like she left to me." Mark responded.

*B*riana sat at the doctor's office and waited for her name to be called. She was nervous to find out her results but she knew she had put herself in this situation. She loved Terrence and she didn't care if it was a possibility that she had HIV.

"Briana Richards," the nurse called back.

She got up and headed to the back.

"Hello sweetie, you're here for your results right," said the nurse.

"Yes, I am," Briana told her.

The nurse looked over her information and then looked back up at Briana.

"Follow me," she said.

The nurse took Briana to one of the rooms.

"The doctor will be in here shortly," the nurse told her.

Briana fumbled with her bag as she waited it seemed like the doctor was taking forever but she finally walked in.

"Hello Briana, how are you?" Dr. Lowe asked.

"I'm fine. I could be better but I'm just so anxious to hear my results," she said.

"Ok, well I've looked them over and I have good news and unwelcome news," she told her.

Briana already had an idea about what the unwelcome news was.

"What's the good news?" she asked.

"Well the good news is that you're going to be a mommy your 3 weeks pregnant," Dr. Lowe told her.

Briana smiled weakly "That's great," she said as she got up to leave.

"Wait, do you wanna know the bad news?" she asked.

Briana looked back "I'm HIV positive," she said and then walked out.

Dr. Lowe ran after Briana "Sweetie this isn't the end of the world," she told her.

"Yes, it is, but I did this to myself so I'm not upset just hurt that I let love get the best of me," she told her.

"Well please tell your partner to come in and get checked as well," the doctor told her.

"No, he doesn't know that he has it," Briana said.

"You do know that it's a crime to pass it around?" said the Dr.

"I didn't give it to him he gave it to me I know the girl he got it from but look ill handle this myself," Briana told her and then walked away.

She walked to the bus stop and broke down crying she was 19 years old pregnant and HIV positive she had ruined her life all because of love. She had a feeling she was pregnant so she already decided to get an abortion but she still had to talk to Terrence. While she was waiting for the bus she saw a black Nissan pull up in front of her.

"You need a ride?" he asked. Briana saw that it was the same guy that had been hanging out with Trina and Terrence.

"Yea sure thanks," she said as she walked over to the car and got in.

"No problem so where you off to?" Donnie asked.

"Home I live a couple blocks away from Trina," Briana told him.

"Ok cool so you and Trina good friends I see?" he asked.

"No. I mean we use to be but not anymore," she told him.

"Why because your fucking Terrence right?" he said with a smile.

Briana looked over at him "I would never do that," she lied.

"Yea I'm sure you won't now if you want your little secret kept with just me. I need you to do me a favor?" he said as he pulled into a dirt road.

Briana got nervous "Look just let me out I'll walk home," she told him.

"Look settle down I'm not going to hurt you now like I was saying if you want your little secret kept quiet then you have to do me a favor," he told her.

"What is that?" she finally answered.

He turned the car off and unzipped his pants and looked at her.

*I*t been almost a week since Desire and Rell spoke. Her phone was blowing up daily everyone was calling her but she never answered. She just needed that alone time. She thought that it was the best way to spend it than with your son. TJ was starting to get irritated.

"I want daddy!" he yelled.

"Ok TJ, but daddy's not here right now," Des told him. She tried to pick him up but he fell out.

"I WANT DADDY, I WANT DADDY!" he screamed.

"TJ please stop! Mommy is going through enough," she said as she pleaded and fought with him.

All he did was kick, and scream. Desire broke down crying

"TJ, STOP IT! STOP IT RIGHT NOW!" Des screamed as she spanked him on his bottom.

TJ burst into tears, Desire was so overwhelmed that she was taking her frustration out on him. Her phone was ringing constantly she just gave up and decided to head back home. She packed their bags and put TJ in the car. She put their bags in the trunk. It seemed liked the ride was longer on their way back.

"I wanna say sorry for spanking you baby mommy is just so overwhelmed, so much has happened this year. Instead of letting this out the right way, I let it build up and get the best of me. Mommy is truly sorry and I hope you can forgive me," Des said to TJ.

The ringing of her phone interrupted her when she looked down she noticed that it was a private call.

"Who the hell is this?" she huffed.

"You been getting set up by Slim since day one," the caller said before hanging up.

Desire looked at her phone she convinced herself that whoever it was had the wrong number. She glanced in the back and TJ was sound asleep. She knew once she got home that Rell was going to be pissed. She no longer cared about his feelings because she saw that he didn't care about hers. As she drove up to the house she saw her uncle's car and Debra's.

"Here we go," she sighed to herself. She parked and woke up TJ.

"Come on we home now so you can see ya dad," she told him as she got him out of the car.

She headed to the door and before she could even grab the knob Rell snatched it open. She was so glad that TJ wasn't in her arms because Rell grabbed her by the neck and lifted her up off the ground

"WHAT THE FUCK IS WRONG WITCHU! ARE YOU FUCKING STUPID?" he yelled.

Desire gasped for air "If you ever pull some stupid shit like that again Desire I swear I'll kill you myself!" he told her.

Mark had given TJ to Debra as he tried to get Rell off Des.

"Get off her brah this ain't the way to this handle shit," he told him.

Desire punched and scratched Rell but her strength was no match to his.

"Let her go son. I know your upset, but I can't and won't let you do this she is still my niece," Robert told him.

Rell finally let go and Desire fell to the ground.

Robert helped her up. "Desire are you ok?" he asked.

She pulled away "I'm fine. Where is my son?" she asked.

"Desire get yourself together first he's fine you both need to stop acting like animals," her uncle told her.

"Fuck you, nigga I'm already seconds off ya ass anyway so just give me a muthafuckin' reason to split ya shit in two," Rell said.

When Desire finally got herself together she was back at it.

"Give me my son," she said as she went towards him.

"Des I'm fareal chill," Rell said as he held his arm out to stop her.

Desire smacked it away "Give me my son you don't deserve to hold him if you can't respect his mother," she said.

Desire kept pushing and smacking Rell's hands out the way, but he finally had enough and gave her the reaction she was looking for.

"Mom take TJ," he told her and Debra did just that.

"Oh, so you bad now huh you feelin' some type of way?" Rell asked as he got in Des' face.

"FUCK YOU!" Desire spat as she slapped him in the face.

"Ok you two stop it," Robert jumped in.

"I'd appreciate it if you backed the fuck off," Rell said without even looking back at him.

Robert backed up but he never sat down "I just think you two need to talk this out. TJ is here and he's safe and so is Desire. Now we need to all think positive this doesn't need to go left," he told them.

"Nigga the word positive shouldn't even be in ya vocabulary," Mark said to him.

He stood up just waiting for Robert to reply. Desire headed to the bedroom and slammed the door. Rell went right behind her.

"Yo, you gotta fuckin' problem?" Rell asked once he entered the room.

Desire ran up without hesitation and punched Rell in his mouth. Rell touched his lip and then looked down at his hand and saw blood. Desire was hype. All the anger she had pent up in her was now coming out. She was dancing around like she was in a boxing ring waiting for the match to start.

"Oh, so you wanna fight" Rell asked.

Desire said nothing and tried to rush Rell again but this time he was on point. He picked her up and slammed her on the bed and got on top of her and pinned her down.

"Get the fuck off me!" Desire yelled as she tried to get up but Rell was too strong.

"Not until you calm down," he told her. Desire tried to bite his hand but he moved his arms away.

"Get off me! Rell I'm not fuckin playing! Get the fuck off me!" she yelled.

Rell still didn't move. Desire was angry and even though he was pissed at her for the stunt she pulled he was still concerned.

"Desire what's wrong with you?" he asked.

She kept trying to fight but she was tiring herself out.

"I just want you to get off me," she told him.

"Desire if you're going to keep trying to fight then nah," Rell told her.

"I'm good," she told him. Rell looked at her but she turned away.

He got off her slowly "I'ma seriously hurt you if you don't calm down," Rell told her. Desire didn't say anything she just went into the bathroom and slammed the door. Rell wanted a response, but deep down inside he didn't need one. He knew that everything was starting to take a toll on Desire.

There was a lot of tension in the air since desire got back, but Rell wasn't bothered by it because he had bigger fish to fry. Mark kept his distance he always had a lot of respect for desire he looked at her like a little sister. So, it was only right that he respected her space until things got better. Debra was hesitant about going on her vacation but Rell told her that he wanted her gone until things simmered down. Desire was barely talking to anyone all her time and attention went on TJ. She didn't sleep in the bedroom and she ignored Rell every chance she got. He tried his best to talk to her and make things right but she wasn't having it. She just got finished cooking dinner when Rell came in from making a run.

"You hungry?" she asked him.

"Yea I am what you cook?" he asked.

"Smothered steak and onions with loaded baked potatoes and salad," she told him.

"Mmm, I missed this you gone fix me a plate?" he asked.

Desire shook her head yes and began fixing the plates. TJ was already in his high chair eating away. They both sat down and said grace before they enjoyed their meal.

"So, you starting your next semester in January?" Rell asked trying to make small talk.

"No, probably February or March," she answered as she took another fork full of her baked potato.

"This food is slammin' bae," he said.

Desire looked up from her plate and at him. Rell knew she was going to say something rude but to his surprise she didn't.

"Someone called me private the day I came back," she told him.

"What did they say?" he asked.

"Something about slim has been setting me up since day one" she told him.

Rell got quiet all the research he had been doing was now falling into place, but he didn't speak on it just yet.

"Don't worry about it they prolli had the wrong number," he told her.

Rell's phone rang which took his attention off the conversation, and whoever he was on the phone with told him some good news because he smiled.

"Who was that?" Des asked.

"You will meet him soon enough," Rell said.

"Ok so what was the phone call all about?" she asked

"Just had to make sure Terrence was still alive," he told her.

Desire didn't know what he was talking about all she knew is that there was a possibility that she didn't have to worry about him anymore and that made her a little happy. But she still had Trina and detective Johnson to worry about so things still were not peaches and cream.

"So, what about detective Johnson any more news on him?" she asked.

"I haven't heard anything yet but hopefully I hear something soon," Rell lied.

"I can't wait until he gets wats coming to that ass," Desire said.

"He won't be the only one," Rell said.

"You one bitch ass nigga," Terrence spat as blood leaked from his mouth.

"Oooh, I'ma bitch nigga because I can finally fight back but it was all good when I couldn't huh," Tyquan said to Terrence.

"Man fuck you, you still a little bitch ass nigga you still aint shit," he told him.

"Yea I'm sure so this what we gone do until bro come here and kill you I figure I do a little torching to you myself dig it."

Terrence didn't answer he watched as the man in front of him grabbed a blow torch. He knew all the shit he had done in his past was now about to bite him dead in the ass.

"Hmmm what should I burn off first your fingers, nah maybe ya eye balls yea that will work," Tyquan said as he got closer to him.

Terrence knew he had to think fast he didn't know how long he was there for but he knew it was for more than a week or so. He was weak and he smelled bad from pissing and shitting on himself. All he wanted to do was get far away from jersey he waited until Tyquan got close enough and then kicked him with all his might. He flew back and hit his head on the table and was out cold from the impact. Terrence started pulling his hand out the rope harder and harder to get it loose. After about 5 minutes he finally got one hand free he was in pain because he had rope burns on his hand but he didn't care he just wanted to get the hell up out of there. He undid his other hand and got up. He almost fainted by the smell and sight of the chair. He wanted to kill Tyquan so bad but he didn't have the strength to. But he made a mental not that if he ever saw him again he would make him suffer. He looked for his gun but he couldn't find it "fuck it" he said to himself as he ran as fast as he could out of the house. He looked around but his car was nowhere in sight. Terrence saw the white navigator but he didn't have the keys and he wasn't taking any chances with going back into the house so he ran over to the driver's side window and smashed it open. He reached in and unlocked the door. He got in the car and tried to hotwire it after almost 3 tries it finally started. As he drove he thought about Briana

"I know that bitch set me up," he said out loud.

He was done with Jersey for now he was going back to Philly where he was comfortable at and didn't need to look over his shoulder the whole time, but he was going to make sure Briana felt pain and nothing but pain the next time they crossed paths. That was something his mother taught him was to never trust women because the only thing they wanted was money and good dick. Terrence always listened to his mother she taught him about life and how it was in the real world. She told him that the only way to get respect is to take it and that was Terrence's motto he always took what he thought belonged to him but as time went on he seen that all the problems he had in life was created by his mother. He was just steps away from meeting death and it was all because the stuff he done to help his mother in the past was coming back 10 times folds.

*D*esire sat at the table looking through an old lock box that her uncle gave her. There were photos of her parents and old letters she was hoping she would find something that could let her know how she was involved in everything that was going on. She got up and answered it

"Hey Debra," Desire said excitedly.

"Hey sweetie, how are you?" she asked.

"I'm good I didn't expect to see you here," Desire said.

"And why is that?" Debra asked.

"Because I thought you would have stayed on your vacation a little longer," Desire said.

"Yea well I got bored and I missed my grandson," Debra said as she sat down.

Desire grabbed two bottled waters out of the fridge she walked over and handed Debra one and then sat down.

"What's all this?" she asked.

"Just some old pictures and letters of my parents. I wanted to ask you something so I'm glad you're here," Desire said.

"What's that baby?" Debra asked.

"Well I noticed that you're no longer Terrence's target. Before it was you and Rell now it's just Rell," Desire said.

"He only wanted to kill me because of his mother. Whatever my sister tells him to do he does it," Debra told her.

"You might be right. I mean whenever me and Rell talk about why him and Terrence is beefing it always adds up to the same thing," Desire said.

Desire couldn't believe what her eyes were seeing when she came across the next stack of pictures.

"What's wrong sweetie?" Debra asked

"He...he knows my mother," Des told her.

"Who?" asked Debra.

Desire didn't answer her she just continued to go through the box. She found a piece of paper that had a P.O box number written on it she wasn't up to finding out any sadder news so she decided to call her uncle and tell him what she had just found.

"What did he say?" Debra asked after Desire got off the phone.

"He said he will be over here soon," Des told her.

About 10 minutes later Rell and TJ walked in desire was so happy to see him because she was so confused at this point.

"Hey babe," he greeted her as he walked in.

"Hey," she said back dryly.

"Mom what you doing here?" he asked.

"Oh, just keeping Desire company," Debra told him.

"You're supposed to be on vacation," he told her.

When Rell looked over at desire he seen a worried look on her face and it concerned him

"Baby what's wrong," he asked.

"Rell this situation is deeper than we think," Des told him.

"What are you talking about?" he asked.

"He knows my mother. Detective Johnson knows my mother," Desire said as she showed him the pictures.

The pictures showed Marie and Donnie hugged up and holding hands. Some pictures even showed them kissing they looked so happy. Rell couldn't believe what he was seeing he was more focused on how much desire looked like her mother the only difference was that Marie was light skinned.

"Did you know they were together?" Rell asked.

"Maybe they were just friends," Desire said trying to convince herself. Rell looked at her seriously

"Bae, they were together at one point and there's no denying that and maybe that's why you're in this. Maybe he's retaliating on you for something your mother did to him god rest her soul," Rell said.

Desire looked at the picture for what seemed like an eternity she wouldn't bring herself to believe that her mother was ever with someone else besides her father.

"Well I'm not going to jump to any conclusions," Desire said.

They all turned their attention to the knock at the door.

"That's probably my uncle," Desire said as she headed to the door.

"Hey unc," she said as she greeted him with a hug.

"Hey, how are you?" he asked.

"I could be better look let's cut the small talk was your partner and my mother together," asked Des.

Robert looked confused "What do you mean together?" he asked.

Desire walked into the kitchen and grabbed the photos.

"Look at this, now if you know anything you should tell me now," Des told him.

Robert looked at the photos and he acted just as shocked as everyone else.

"Desire I'm not sure what to tell you but this is all new to me," said Robert.

"So, you don't know anything at all" she asked again.

"No, I don't and if I did I would have been told you," said Robert.

"I also found this maybe this is the answer to everything," Des said as she handed him the piece of paper with the P.O box number on it.

"Desire we will have to go back to Jersey you know that right," Robert told her.

"Yea I know," she said.

"Well look, how about we all go back I mean we're stronger together than by our self," Debra said.

"Nah, I don't need yawl in the cross fire if shit pops off," Rell told her.

"Look, if we're here or in Jersey they will still find us and start some shit so why not go back together," Debra said.

"I mean she's right," said Robert.

Rell gave he a shut the fuck up look and Robert caught on and did exactly that. Before he could speak his cell went off. Desire could tell something was wrong by the scowl on his face she knew something had happened.

"Baby what's wrong?" she asked. Rell ended the call.

"Yawl ready to ride out?" he asked them.

Everyone looked at each other and nodded their heads.

*T*rina turned over and snuggled up under Donnie he sighed loudly which made her look at him.

"What's wrong with you?" she asked.

"I'm tryna figure out why you laying on me?" he told her.

Trina sat up "Oh, so it's like that but you weren't just saying that when you were fucking me in my ass," she yelled.

Donnie sat up slowly his tall lanky body still towered over Trina and he wasn't even standing up. He looked at her and smile she looked at him confused but before she could respond he grabbed her by the throat.

"Listen here you little bitch. The only reason I even came back into your life is because I wanted Desire dead and Tyshawn wants Rell dead so don't ever think for one second that I'm here for you. Just because we fuck doesn't mean a damn thing," Donnie said as he roughly let her go.

Trina winced in pain as she rubbed her neck.

"I have my reasons why I wanted Desire dead. What's yours and who is Tyshawn?" she asked.

Donnie lit up a cigar laid back and put his hand behind his head.

"Because she was a part of James and I hated that man with everything inside me," he told her.

"Why the hell you hate him?" she asked.

"Because he took Marie away from me. She fell in love with him and had his baby," Donnie told her.

"So, after everything me and you been through with you being in and out of my life it's still just fuck me, right? You're only here for a dummy mission and then you're gone again and you never told me who Tyshawn was?" Trina said.

Donnie checked his cell and then put it back down.

"First of all, I couldn't tolerate the shit you were doing back then and me and James didn't see eye to eye so fuck yea I didn't come around and Tyshawn is Terrell's father," said Donnie.

"I'm not understanding," Trina said.

Donnie shook his head and put out his cigar "Me and Tyshawn go way back we lost contact and the first time I saw him again was a few years ago. I remember this day because he was beat up pretty bad he told me that him and Terrell got into it over his brother Tyquan. He knew how I was back in the day so he asked me if I could handle it. I told him that I would get back to him but I quickly agreed once I found out that Terrell and Desire was together shit I can kill two birds with one stone," Donnie boosted.

Trina laughed she couldn't believe how much she enjoyed being around this man.

"Well desire is dead thank god now all we have to do is go after Rell and who is Tyquan because all I know about is Terrence and Terrell," she asked.

"Tyquan is their little brother he's a couple years younger than them I think, but none of that matters right now," he said as he pulled

Trina close and guided her head down to his dick. It was limp so Trina took him into her hands and jerked up and down slowly. She teased the head with her tongue until she finally became erect. She took him into her mouth and didn't stop until she reached his balls.

"Shit, you always could suck a mean dick," he moaned.

Trina laughed and continued to do what she did best.

*I*t had been a week since they came back to jersey and they had to lay low until they made their next move. They all stayed in a small home in Buena NJ that Robert had rented. He was making all the plans and telling everyone what to do. Rell and mark wasn't feeling that so they started doing things their way.

"Ight yawl stay here we gotta go make a few runs," Rell said.

"When will you be back?" asked Des.

"Soon just make sure you keep TJ safe ok?" he said as he kissed her on the forehead.

Desire nodded as she watched them leave.

"I can't wait until all this is over. I prayed that yawl would never have to go through this again," Debra said.

"I've heard and seen a lot of stuff while being with slim oh I mean Robert, but I must say that this here is all new to me family vs. family," Mattie said.

Debra raised her eyebrow at Mattie, but she didn't respond. Desire rubbed TJ's head as she sat quietly thinking about her next move. She knew it could either cost her, her life or jail time so she had to think smart. Either way she was going to seek out what needed to be done.

"This shit can't be real," Rell snapped.

"I don't understand why he never told me. I mean I brought Donnie around before and introduced him as my partner neither one of them said anything to me," said Robert.

"All I know is that Desire is gonna be pissed and hurt all in one and the sad part about it is that she can't go to her parents and ask them why," Rell said as he shook his head.

After Rell and Robert checked out the P.O box they found out that it belonged to desire's mother and that she was hiding a secret that desire should've been known about a long time ago. The only thing that Rell didn't like was the fact that Robert gave desire the lock box that he claimed he never opened

"So, who will tell her me or you?" Robert asked.

"I'll tell her," Rell said.

"This shit is crazy man like it seems like more shit keeps pushing its way to the surface Ima start popping any nigga that makes me feel uncomfortable," Mark said as he looked at Robert.

Rell was lost in his thoughts as he drove.

"Where are we going son?" Robert asked.

"I gotta go meet somebody," Rell told him.

Robert looked at Rell suspiciously wondering who he could be meeting around here. After driving for almost 30 minutes they pulled up to a corner store.

"Muthafucka you mean to tell me you drove for 30 minutes just to come to a fuckin store shit I better see Michael Jackson moon walk outta that bitch," Mark huffed.

Robert laughed but Rell didn't he just picked up his cell and call someone.

"I'm outside," was all he said before he ended the call.

Rell waited until he seen Tyquan come out. He wore a grey and black sweat suit with black timberlands. He had a muscular frame with broad shoulders. His curly hair was pulled back into a bushy pony tail. His butterscotch complexion glowed from the bright sunlight.

"Get out," Rell told Robert and mark.

They both looked at him Rell didn't repeat his self he just got out the car and walked over to him.

"So, what happened?" Rell asked Tyquan

"Man, I don't know everything was going as planned but he still got away," he told Rell.

"Bullshit you fucked up because you tried to do shit your way," Rell told him, Mark walked up with a surprised look on his face.

"Man, I know this ain't Tyquan?" he asked.

"Yea this him," said Tell.

"Damn nigga you all grown now," Mark said as he playfully hit him.

"Yea man I am," said Tyquan.

Robert stood there clueless he saw that the guy was a spitting image of Terrell "Who is this?" Robert asked.

"This ma lil bro," he told Robert.

Tyquan gave him a nod because he wasn't really feeling his presence.

"It's nice to meet you," Robert told him.

"Ok well enough of the meet and greet Terrence is still out there," Rell said.

"Look I say we hold off on his ass and go after des sister and that nigga Donnie," Mark stated.

"Nah I'm tryna take them all out at once," Rell said.

"**B**itch what the fuck do you want?" Trina barked as she answered the door.

"We need to talk," Briana said as she walked in.

"About what?" she asked as she sat down on her sofa.

"Look Trina me and Terrence been sleeping around and I'm pregnant," Briana blurted out.

Trina gave her an evil look "Bitch, are you fuckin' stupid you been sleeping with my man!" Trina yelled and then got up.

Briana took a step back "He's not your man Trina you're in denial and he's not my man either but what I do know is that I am pregnant by him and I also have HIV and I got it from Terrence," Briana told her.

Trina walked up on Briana slowly and Briana started backing up more.

"He is my man and its hoes like you that make it hard for women like me you a trifling bitch! Talking about you're my friend, bitch friends don't fuck each other's boyfriends," Trina said.

Briana looked at her in disgust "Are you kidding me? You wanna talk about friendship, but the whole time you were fucking my father and you gave him aids too, and I'm gonna tell Terrence to get checked because I know for a fact that he gave it to me," Briana told her.

"Bitch, you're not telling him anything!" Trina yelled as she pushed Briana into the wall.

Briana punched Trina in the face which made her stumble back she tried to make a run for the door but Trina grabbed her by her hair.

"Bitch you ain't going nowhere," Trina said as threw Briana on the floor.

Briana knew that Trina wasn't a fighter but she also didn't want to risk losing her baby. She tried to get up but Trina kicked her in the stomach.

"You lying bitch," Trina spat as she kicked her again.

Briana held her stomach as a sharp pain hit her. She waited until Trina tried to kick her again and she grabbed her leg and bit down hard.

"Aahhhhhhhhhh!" Trina yelled as she fell to the ground.

Briana gained enough strength to get up she walked over to Trina as she held her stomach.

"Punk bitch," Briana yelled as she kicked Trina in her stomach.

"I hate you for ruining my life I hope desire kills your conniving ass!" she yelled as she kicked her repeatedly.

Briana had, had enough she was done with all the drama that Trina had involved her in. she quickly left out of Trina's house and got back into her father's car. Tears ran down her face as she drove home she no longer wanted that weight on her shoulders. She pulled up to her house and got out of the car. She went inside and saw her mother's frail body sitting in the chair smoking a cigarette. Her mother smiled at her weakly but Briana turned her head and headed upstairs to her bedroom. She sat down on her bed and got out a pen and paper from her night stand. She decided to write Terrence a letter that read:

*if you're reading this then I'm probably already dead I found out that I was pregnant and HIV positive all in one day. I wanted to tell you as soon as I found out but I was scared so I confronted the person who gave it to you *Trina*. I revealed to her that we have been sleeping together for some time now and she blew a fuse. Things went left because I also told her that I was going to tell you* *the truth about everything and we got into a fight finally able to get away from her I realized that I no longer wanted to do this. All the drama that's been going on in my life is too much and I refuse to bring a child into this mess. I'm tired of carrying this burden I'm ready to be set free. I hope Trina get what's coming to her and I hope desire is the one that does it. Well I guess there's not much else to say except I love you and I always have. Don't worry I'll be watching over you to make sure you stay out of trouble. Good bye Terrence, love Briana.*

After she finished writing the letter she folded it up and put it in an envelope. Briana wrote Terrence name and address on the front she went downstairs and left out. She shoved the letter half way in the mailbox so the mailman would know to take it. She went back into the house and back upstairs. Briana went into the bathroom and ran a bath she stripped herself naked and looked in the mirror. She put her hands on her stomach "please forgive mommy" she said and then opened the medicine cabinet. She grabbed her father's blade that he shaved his head with. She walked over and got into the tub slowly. She closed her eyes as tears ran down her face "paradise here I come," she said and then she ran the blade across her throat.

Desire wasn't going to waste any more time she had been waiting for hours for Rell to get back. It was late and she wasn't waiting any longer. She made sure TJ was tucked in bed sound asleep before she made her move. Desire stood in the mirror dressed in all black she made sure her hat was low and her hoody was tied tight. She looked in Rell's duffle bag and grabbed his 9mm. she crept slowly out of the bedroom and bumped directly into Debra.

"What are you doing?" she whispered.

"The question is where are you going?" Debra asked.

"I'm going to look for Trina," Desire responded.

Debra knew desire was stubborn so she didn't even try to stop her.

"Earlier when we was talking did you hear how Mattie called ya uncle by a different name?" Debra asked.

Desire thought on it for a second "Yea why?" she asked.

"Something ain't right Desire," Debra told her.

Desire agreed, but she couldn't put her focus on anything else

"Look after TJ and if anything, pop off you shoot first and ask questions later," Desire said as she grabbed her uncle's keys off the hook and disappeared into the night.

Desire took her time making it to Trina's she thought about everything she took her through. An image of a burned down house appeared in her head. She wanted to make sure that she wouldn't regret what she was about to do but the more she thought the more she didn't care. It only took her a half hour to get to stony brook apartments. When she pulled up to Trina's apartment something didn't sit right with her. Once desire was out of the car she was grabbed from behind she had been caught slipping.

*I*t was late when they got back to the house they all lost track of time because they were trying to figure out how they could end everything once and for all. When they pulled up Robert noticed his car was gone, but he didn't say anything. when Rell came in he headed straight for the bedroom he knew desire was probably worried so he wanted to let her know that he was ok. When he walked in the bedroom he only saw TJ tucked in bed sound asleep. He walked back out and went into the room where his mother was sleeping

"Mom where Des at?" he asked as he shook her gently.

"She should be sleeping we all laid down around the same time," she lied.

He went back out into the living room where Robert, Mark, and Tyquan waited.

"Desire's gone she's not here," he told them.

"I know I seen that my car was gone when we pulled up," Robert said in a disappointed tone.

Rell thought for a second and then ran back to the room he looked in his duffle bag and seen that his 9mm was gone.

"FUCK!" he said out loud.

By this time Mattie was up and concerned, but Debra had already peeped game.

"What's going on?" Debra asked as Rell came back into the living room.

"She's going after Trina she took my gun," Rell said.

"Well shit let's ride out," said Tyquan.

"Yawl stay here and make sure all windows and doors are locked," Robert told them.

They wasted no time hopping in the car and speeding off "So where she at bro?" Tyquan asked.

Rell ignored him and picked up his cell to call desire, she wasn't answering which made him even more worried because he didn't know if something happened to her. All he could do was picture desire laid on the floor in a pool of blood and seeing Trina or Terrence standing over her with their gun drawn. He quickly erased that image out of his head.

He almost forgot where he was going until Robert grabbed his attention.

"I don't see her car isn't this where Trina lives?" He asked

Rell pulled into the apartment complex and looked around.

"That's Trina's apartment right there," Rell said.

Robert grabbed his gun "Stay here I'm going to go look around," he told them as he got out of the car.

He walked up slowly to her doorstep he wiggled the knob and it was unlocked. He slowly walked in with his gun drawn he heard no noises and the place was quiet. He was headed down the hallway when he slipped on something wet he looked down and saw blood he panicked thinking desire might be dead in one of the rooms. He started kicking the doors of each room in hoping he saw someone to put a hole in. after he realized no one was there he left out. He ran back to the car and got in

"The apartment is empty but there's blood on the floor," he told them.

Rell hit the steering wheel "FUCK! MAN, I SWEAR IF SOMETHING HAPPEN TO DESIRE IMA KILL ALL THEM MUTHAFUCKA'S!" he yelled angrily.

"Calm down bro ain't nothing gone happen to sis," said Tyquan.

Mark sat in the back making sure his gun was loaded he was a quiet one but he was not someone you wanted to cross.

"We will find her don't worry," Robert told him in a calm tone.

Mark sucked his teeth and Tyquan cleared his throat at Robert's comment. Rell laid his head on the steering wheel he wished that desire didn't go off the way she did everything was happening back to back and it was beginning to be too much for him. His mind was everywhere and he couldn't focus straight but then something hit him.

"Where did Desire's parents live when she was a teenager?" he asked.

Robert looked at him "Bridgeton it's a small town about 45 minutes from here why?" he asked.

"I know where she is," Rell said.

"Where?" asked Robert.

"She went back home," Rell told them.

"**W**ho are you?" Desire asked the driver.

"Don't worry about all that," he responded.

"Where are you taking me?" she asked.

"To where it all started," he told her.

Desire didn't understand what he was talking about until they pulled up to an abandon burned down house. The man got out of the car and went to the trunk.

"Get outta the car bitch," he spat.

When Desire got out of the car she saw Trina get out of the trunk. Desire didn't know who this guy was, but whoever he was he was way ahead of her.

"You try to run and Ima blow the back of your head off," he warned.

"What the hell are we doing here?" Trina asked once she noticed where she was.

"Shut up don't ask no fuckin questions, now walk," Des told her.

Trina squinted her eyes and then looked as if she had seen a ghost when she finally saw Desire.

"Yea bitch, I'm back," Desire told her.

Trina walked into what was left of an abandoned house. It was cold and dark inside the only light they had was from the street lights.

"I brought you here. Now everything else is on you," the guy told her as he got back into his car and pulled off

"You see what you did Trina?" Desire asked.

Trina smirked "I did a hell of a job for my first time," she said sarcastically.

In the blink of an eye Desire hit Trina across the face with her gun "You heartless bitch! Look around you burned down our house you killed our parents," Desire yelled.

Trina held her face "How many times do I have to tell you that I don't give a flying fuck about none of this? Desire when will you learn that I'm always going to win? I've moved on with my life and yet your still buried in the past because your parents are dead. Get the fuck over it people die every day who gives a fuck!" Trina said as each word flowed like poison off her tongue.

This time Desire hit her much harder with the gun "You evil bitch they were your parents too! And this isn't just about them. Do you realize what I went through after they died? I was homeless, I barely had money for food. I got picked on in school because I didn't have any clothes so I wore the same outfit and, where were you? Out fucking and sucking for money. You got away with murder Trina and people say I'm hateful no one knows the real you but me," Desire said.

Trina wiped the blood from her mouth.

"They weren't my parents and I don't give a damn about what you went through. You deserved every bit of what you got. Always thinking you were better than me; going to school and doing the right thing bitch please," Trina said

"So, you hate me because I actually wanted something out of life? You are crazy, you could of did the same thing I did, but you chose to skip school and run the streets. That's not my problem you went out of your way to make my life a living hell and now I've reached my breaking point," Des told her.

"YOU SUPPOSE TO BE DEAD ANYWAY BITCH!" Trina yelled as she charged Desire.

They both fell to the ground and the gun flew out of desires hand. Desire and Trina both tussled on the floor for the gun. Desire was much stronger than Trina so she pushed her off and she fell back. Desire tried to get up but Trina grabbed her legged and pulled her back down. She jumped on desire's back and wrapped her arm around her neck and held as tight as she could

"I'm going to make sure you die this time. You deserve to be dead bitch, and the best part about everything is that bitch of a mother lied to you. She cheated on your father with my father we're not even real sister's dumb ass! You don't deserve to be happy, I do! I'm the one that needs to be happy! You don't know how it feels for a guy to just fuck you and throw you away like you're a piece of trash! You get a good man on your first try and your ugly and fat bitch die!" Trina yelled as she held on tighter.

Desire was getting light headed she heard a screeching sound and saw car lights. The next thing she saw was 4 men running in.

"GET THE FUCK OFF HER!" Rell yelled as he grabbed Trina by her throat and shoved her off Desire.

Desire gasped for air and tried to regain her strength. Trina tried to get back up but mark pointed his gun at her.

"Give me a reason," he told her.

Trina backed down but didn't take her eyes off him. Robert sat back and watched instead of helping.

"Well, well, well if it isn't my old partner good ol detective Martinez," a voice said from behind.

Everyone turned around and saw Donnie standing there. Without notice Rell rushed him and tackled him to the floor, and started throwing nothing, but left and rights. Each hit connected to his face. With all the attention focused on Donnie and Rell. No one saw Robert slide the gun over to Trina. When mark saw her from the corner of his eye he spun around just in time and raised his gun and gave Trina 3 shots to the stomach.

"You gave me one," he said as he watched her hit the ground.

Donnie was on the ground bleeding from the nose and mouth.

"Let's go. Let's get out of here," Robert told them.

Rell and Tyquan helped desire up and they headed out. Donnie took what strength he had in him to get up he crawled over to where Trina laid and watched her bleed out. He was never really in Trina's life to begin with, but he wasn't going to watch her die. He grabbed the gun and went after Robert.

"UNCLE ROBERT!" Desire called out and he turned around.

Donnie only had a chance to shoot once before Robert dove on him. Robert struggled to get the gun out of Donnie's hands but he wasn't giving up. He finally knocked it out of his hands and tried to choke Donnie. Donnie pushed his thumbs into Robert's eyes and pushed him off.

"Aaahhhh!" Robert yelled.

Donnie crawled for the gun and then stood up but when he got up he felt a burning sensation which knocked him right back down. He tried to get back up but he could no longer move his legs.

"Let's go fareal this time," Rell said.

Robert got up and got himself together. They all got into the car and pulled off.

"Stop right here," Rell said.

Mark pulled over to where Rell was pointing to.

"Give me your guns," Rell told them.

They all gave him their guns and he got out he threw them all in the Cohansey River one by one and then got back into the car.

"She was going to kill me," Desire said just above a whisper.

Rell looked at her "Well she can no longer hurt you anymore," Rell told her.

"Who was the other dude?" Tyquan asked.

"Trina's father," Rell told him.

Desire looked at him "What the hell are you talking about?" she asked.

"Desire, Donnie is Trina's real father. The P.O box number you found was your mother's. It had letters from Donnie in it, and letters to you from your mother in it telling you everything," Rell told her.

Everyone in the car got real quiet. Desire couldn't believe what she had just found out. She started putting all the pieces together and everything now made since. She still didn't know who the man was who grabbed her, but whoever he was knew about everything. Through the whole ride desire was lost in her thoughts she cried silent tears as she thought about her mother. She thought she told her everything but it appears her mother hid a lot from her. Desire knew sooner or later that anymore unanswered questions that she had would soon come out because whatever happens in the dark will soon come to the light.

Two weeks since the incident Desire found herself cleaning house. She tried to forget about that night and she didn't have a care in the world about what happened to Trina or Donnie. Desire had burned everything of Trina and her parents. She no longer wanted any dealings with her past she was moving on and setting herself free.

"What's going on out here?" Rell asked when he came out on the deck.

He spotted Desire standing over the grill and throwing things on it.

"Oh, just nothing," she told him.

Rell looked at her.

"Ok, so you throwing pictures and clothes on a lit grill ain't nothing?" he asked.

Desire chuckled "Well I guess that it something," she said.

"Yea I guess so to so tell me what all this is about?" he asked.

"Well I'm just ready to move on I'm getting rid of everything of my parents and Trina and I'm just going to move on with my life," she told him.

Rell shook his head "I agree it's time for us both to move on," he told her.

She threw the last of the items on the grill and her and Rell watched them burn.

"So, I wanted to talk to you about something," Des told him. Rell walked back into the house and she followed.

"What's that?" he asked as he went in the fridge and grabbed a bottled water.

"Tyquan where the hell did he come from?" Des asked.

Rell sipped his water and took a seat at the table.

"I was hoping you forgot about seeing him I mean it's been 2 weeks since you saw him," Rell said.

Desire sat down and looked at him "You know I don't forget anything. So, why didn't you tell me about him?" she asked.

"Because there wasn't anything to tell," Rell said.

"Seriously, so you having another brother wasn't important," she asked.

Rell took another sip of his water and shook his head.

"Nah, I'm not saying that. All I'm saying is that the timing wasn't right. I mean, I was going to tell you eventually," he told her.

Desire got up and walked over to the kitchen counter she grabbed one of her sharp cutting knives and walked over to where Rell was sitting. He took another sip of his water and then did a double take

"Yo, Des what the fuck you doing?" Rell asked as he jumped out of the chair

"Why you running? I mean you steady hiding shit, and then you wanna make up an excuse," Desire said as she walked closer to him.

"Oh, so you gone cut me for not telling you I had another brother? I mean damn a nigga thought the timing was bad shit," he pleaded.

"You so full of shit," she told him as she went to put the knife back.

"I'm serious babe I was going to tell you but it just wasn't the right time you know I'll tell you anything," Rell said.

"Rell you tell me stuff when you get ready, but whatever I'm trying to put all the bullshit behind me so if you bullshit then you left behind me," she told him before walking out of the kitchen.

*S*he stood in the mirror looking at her bruised and blemished face. She couldn't stand to look at how wore out she was so she turned around and went back out to her room. She winced in pain as she climbed back into the bed.

"Mrs. Boyd, are you ready for your pain medicine?" the nurse asked.

Trina looked at her and waved her away "I'm not taking no fucking medicine just let me go home," Trina said.

The nurse shook her head "Sweetie, I've been taking care of you for 2 weeks and you are the most miserable person I've ever seen. I'm not one to judge, but I bet that hole in your stomach happened because of your ways," the nurse told her.

Trina turned her head so fast that she almost snapped her neck "Bitch, you don't know shit about me. Now get the fuck on before you get spit on," Trina snapped.

The nurse sighed "That attitude ain't going to get you nowhere honey mark my words. You live by the sword and you're going to die by it; God don't like ugly," the nurse told her and left out of the room.

Trina was heated she wanted to go after the nurse but she was in too much pain. She looked over to see if the nurse had left her pain medicine but she didn't.

"Broke bitch," Trina spat as she buzzed the nurses' station.

The lady was right about god don't like ugly because no one came to check on Trina and throughout the day the pain in her stomach got worse. She buzzed the nurses' station again and again but still no one came. Eventually after an hour had passed Trina saw the nurse from earlier walk pass

"NURSE!" she called out.

The lady stopped and walked back into her room.

"Yes, do you want something?" asked the nurse.

Trina held her stomach "Please can you give me my pain meds," she begged as she winced in pain.

The nurse smiled "Now why should I help you and you were so rude to me?" she asked.

"Just because I'm unhappy I shouldn't have taken it out on you. Now can you please give me my medicine?" Trina asked again.

The nurse nodded and walked over to her "You see what you just said? Just because your unhappy that you shouldn't have taken it out on me? Well, that's how you should treat everyone including your family. Just because you made the choices you made doesn't mean you make others suffer because your life is in shambles," the nurse told her as she put the medicine her Trina's IV.

Trina looked up at the nurse and eyed her strangely.

"What's your name?" she asked.

"It took you 2 weeks to realize that you didn't know my name?" the nurse asked.

"Well, I've been in my own little world I guess," Trina told her.

"Indeed, you have, and its Marie by the way. Now you're going to get sleepy because I gave you a stronger dose but the pain should be gone for a few hours," the nurse told her.

Trina looked at the nurse when she told her what her name was. She noticed that the nurse looked familiar but she didn't say anything about it.

"Ok now you get some rest honey," the nurse told her and then started to walk away.

Trina laid back and closed her eyes she thought about the nurse and knew she looked familiar and then it hit her.

"Nurse, nurse," she called out but no one came.

She buzzed the nurses' station again and again until a nurse came.

"Girl what is wrong with you buzzing that damn thing like you're crazy?" asked a ghetto white nurse.

Trina ignored her rudeness "Can you please tell Nurse Marie that I need her?" Trina said.

The lady looked at her like she had lost her mind.

"Girl what? Don't nobody by that name work here," the nurse told her.

Trina looked confused "She has been caring for me for 2 weeks you must be new because she works here," Trina told her.

The nurse rolled her eyes.

"Little girl, I've been working here for 5 years and I have yet to see a lady named Marie work here. So, either you're crazy or them pain meds got you tripping," the nurse told her and then stormed away.

Trina's mind was everywhere she knew someone had to see that lady. But she was wrong because every nurse that passed her room she asked them about her and they all told her the same thing there was no nurse named Marie that worked there.

"**H**APPY NEW YEAR!" everybody screamed when the ball dropped. Everything was going good desire and Rell decided to have a little get together. Desire thought it was just for New Year's but Rell had other plans in mind.

"Desire comes on out here so we can get this dance circle going," Debra yelled from the bedroom.

"I'm coming now," she said as she washed her hands.

"Come on girl just because I'm 46 don't mean I can't still move," Debra said as she started dropping it low.

Desire burst into laughter "You better stop now," she told her.

They both went out into the living room and started dancing. Rell, Mark, and Tyquan all sat and had a few drinks as they watched the ladies dance.

"Yo bro can I holla at you for a second?" Tyquan asked.

"Yea let's go sit on the deck," Rell told him. They went on the deck and sat down.

"Wassup bro?" Rell asked.

"How long we gone let this shit ride out for" he asked.

"Not for too much longer," Rell told him.

"Cool because I'm ready to off this shady ass nigga," Tyquan told him.

"I feel you I'm just tryna make sure shit play out right so don't worry about nothing just keep ya guard up iight," Rell said.

"No doubt we in this together bro," Tyquan told him.

"Cool now let's get back inside," Rell told him.

Once they were inside Rell poured everyone a glass of wine and handed it to them.

"Can I have everyone's attention please?" Rell asked.

Everyone looked towards him and Debra cut off the music.

"First and foremost, I would like to say happy new years to all of yawl. I wanna thank yawl for being there for me and Desire through all the good, and tough times; we truly appreciate it. I hope this year is much better for all of us," he said and they all raised their glasses and toasted.

Rell gulped down his glass of wine and sat it on the table.

"I have one more announcement," Rell said.

He turned to Des and grabbed her hands; she looked into his eyes, and he looked into hers.

"Desire, from the first day I saw you I knew that we was gonna be together. You been riding with me since day one, and I love you for that. You gave me my first child and son, you dealt with all the groupie ass girls that wouldn't leave our relationship alone, and you dealt with some disloyal ass niggas who I thought was my homies. You suffered physically, and mentally from some of the shit we been through and so did TJ. I want yawl both to know how much I love yawl. No matter what you may think Desire my love and loyalty is to you and TJ. I'm not going anywhere no time soon. The only thing that will separate me and you is God taking me off this earth," Rell said.

Mark glanced over at Robert and Mattie and seen that they were whispering to each other. He nudged Tyquan and he peeped it too. Desire was already in tears everything that Rell said was from the heart and it made everything they had been through worth it. Rell took a box out of his pocket and got on one knee. Desire put her hands over her mouth.

"Desire Marie Boyd will you marry me?" he asked.

She looked down at the ring with teary eyes and smiled.

"Yes, Terrell Williamson I will marry you," she said and he placed the ring on her finger.

Everyone clapped and cheered while Desire and Rell hugged and kissed. It was a beautiful moment. Desire couldn't believe she was married after everything she been through. God showed her everything happened for a reason. She had her family and she was now going to be a wife. She had no idea Rell was going to propose to her, but she was glad that holding him down for almost 4 years had paid off.

"**D**o Terrence still live in Philly?" Tyshawn asked Robert.

"You will have to ask Diane about that," Robert responded as he took a sip of his beer.

"Cool, so how you been Mattie?" Tyshawn asked.

"I've been better," she responded.

"Things have been going real smooth lately I see," he told them.

"Yea, after all of this is over me and Mattie is going to take a much-needed vacation," said Robert.

Tyshawn took a pull of his cigarette and then put it out.

"Check this, I need a few dollars," he said to Robert.

Robert blew loudly. "How much money have I given you already?" he asked.

"It don't matter motherfucker I need more," Tyshawn snapped.

Robert pulled out his check book and wrote Tyshawn a check. "Here now I think it's time for you to go," said Robert.

Tyshawn smiled as he got up.

"I'll see you soon," he said before he walked out.

"**H**appy anniversary beautiful," Desire opened her eyes and was greeted by Rell and a dozen of roses.

"Happy anniversary baby and thank you," desire said as she got up and took the roses.

"TJ is with mommy so we got the day all to ourselves and we can do whatever you want," Rell told her.

"I just wanna make love all day long," Desire told him.

Rell got undressed and slid in bed "Your wish is my command," he said as he got on top of des.

She welcomed Rell's dick inside her with no problem. As his dick disappeared in and out of her she thought about everything that went on in the last couple years and she was truly happy with the outcome. She truly loved Rell and she was glad he was in her life.

"I love you Mr. Williamson," Desire said.

"I love you too Mrs. Williamson," Rell said back and they did exactly what Desire wanted made love all day long.

As they sat and held each other Desire wondered was this really the end of the madness; she wondered was this their happily ever after.

"Baby, do you think we could finally be happy now," Desire asked.

Rell brushed her hair back with his hand.

"Honestly, Desire I don't know because it's a lot of undercover shit going on," Rell told her.

"Like what?" she asked.

"I can't speak on it right now," Rell said to her.

Just by that statement Desire knew that their happiness would soon be interrupted.

"Terrell this is bullshit I mean I don't understand why we can't just enjoy life minus the bullshit," Desire said.

Rell gave her a serious look. "I'ma make sure you and TJ don't have to go through no more bullshit believe that," Rell stated.

*D*esire moved around the kitchen trying to finish up dinner the New Year was starting off pretty good. The only sad thing was that she had just found out about Briana committing suicide. Even though Briana tried to set Desire up she still felt bad. Rell sat on the floor in the living room with TJ playing with toys. The smell of curry chicken filled the room which made his stomach growl even more because that was one of his favorite dishes.

"Daddy I got go pee," TJ said to him. Rell smiled he was so proud of how well TJ was talking he thought with all the drama that went on in the previous year would affect him but it didn't. Him and Desire finally had time to enjoy life and be parents.

"Iight come on," he said as he took TJ to the bathroom.

TJ took down his pull up and climbed on the toilet. Rell stood by the door until TJ was finished. He busted out laughing when TJ reached down grabbed his penis and shook it. TJ jumped off the toilet and pulled up his pull up. He flushed the toilet

"Daddy wash hands," he said.

Rell picked TJ up and turned on the water TJ washed his hands and then shook them wildly.

"You good now," Rell asked as he put him down.

"Yea," he said and ran back into the living room.

Rell shook his head because TJ was a spitting image of him. It made him feel good that he was raising him right. Rell walked into the kitchen and wrapped his arms around Desire's stomach.

"Rell stop," Desire said as he kissed on her neck

"You know you don't want me to stop," he told her.

"Yes, I do because TJ watches everything you do," she told him.

Desire was right because TJ watched in awe as his parents kissed like tomorrow would never come.

"Mommy I want kiss," TJ said running into the kitchen.

Desire and Rell both looked at him.

"Ok mommy give you kiss," Desire said as she tried to peck him on the lips.

TJ grabbed the back of her head.

"Wait TJ no you can't kiss mommy like that," Desire said as she pulled away.

She looked back and Rell was bent over laughing.

"That is not funny now is the time to talk to him about not doing the things you do," Desire told him.

After nearly 5 minutes Rell finally got himself together.

"Iight lil man the things you see daddy do to mommy you can't do because that's your mother and next lil kids shouldn't be doing that," Rell told him.

"Ok," TJ responded.

"Now, you're not in trouble but me and your mother is together. Now once you grow up and get ya own place and get you a girl then you can grab her ass and kiss her all you want, but this right here is mines," Rell told him as he smacked Desire on her ass.

Desire just looked at him. "Seriously Rell," she said.

"What? Shit you gotta be honest with him," Rell told her.

"Yea but that was too honest. TJ, you just can't do certain things and you're not in trouble we just need you to know that the things we do or the things daddy does to me are things you can't do. Especially to me, now once you're a little bit older we will explain more to you about things like this ok." Desire said.

"Ok mommy," said TJ.

"Yea you can't do everything I do because everything I do is not good ok lil man?" Rell asked

"Ok daddy," TJ responded.

"Ok now yawl go sit down while I fix the plates," she told them.

Rell put TJ in his high chair and then sat down. Desire fixed their plates and gave it to them she went back to fix hers and then came back and sat down. They said grace and then started to eat.

"TJ make sure you blow your food because it's hot," Des told him.

"Damn bae this is good," Rell said.

"Thanks bae I taste it getting better and better every time I cook it," Desire said.

"Yea I feel you," Rell said

They ate dinner and made conversation and Afterwards Rell helped Desire clean up and then he gave Rell told him as he put him in the bed and tucked him in.

"Night daddy," said TJ

"Good night lil man," Rell said and kissed him on the cheek.

He went into the bedroom where he saw Desire putting on one of his big t shirts.

"Ima hop in the shower real quick, put on a movie," he told her and went in the bathroom.

Desire climbed into bed and turned on the T.V she browsed through the guide until she found a good movie. After 20 minutes Rell came out of the bathroom wrapped in a towel.

He dried off put on his boxers and slid into bed.

"What we watchin'?" he asked.

"Friday," she told him

"This ma shit," Rell said as he laid down and wrapped his arms around des.

"Rell what ever happened to Kevin?" she asked.

"Kevin who?" he faked like he didn't know.

Desire sat up and looked at him. "Kevin your boy or should I say use to be your boy," Desire said.

"Nah, I don't know no Kevin. The only Kevin I know died in a freak accident a lil bit ago now go to sleep," Rell told her.

Desire laid back down and drifted off to sleep. Rell tossed and turned all night he broke into cold sweats and had one bad dream after another. He finally opened his eyes and starred at the ceiling he managed to slide from underneath desire and get out of the bed. He went to the kitchen to get himself something cold to drink and sat down at the table. He thought about his mother; he always had dreams of his mother touching him on his privates when he was just a little boy and her beating him when he said he would tell. She made his life hell and he didn't know what to do or who to talk to. He loved Desire dearly, but he didn't want her looking at him funny. At times, he wanted to tell Debra but he knew that would break her heart so he kept it in. finally he picked up the house phone and dialed Tyquan's number.

"Yo, what up ma bad to call you so late," he said.

"Nah you good wassup man?" Tyquan asked.

"I'm having them nightmares again. I don't understand why they just won't stop," he said.

"Damn bro you talked to anybody about it?" he asked.

"No, I don't need anybody knowing that mommy use to touch me," he told him.

"Bro you gotta do watchu gotta do to put this shit behind you. I know watchu going through daddy use to beat the shit out of me when I was staying with him. Even after I got my own place I would still have visions of him walking through the door drunk at night and cracking me over my head with a beer bottle while I was sleeping. I'm always looking over my shoulder like someone is out to get me but I'm dealing with it," Tyquan told him.

Rell got quiet all he wanted to do was live a normal life and he couldn't even do that. He had completely turned his life around and yet his past was still haunting him.

"I don't know man I'm just so tired of all this, like damn can't a nigga just be happy man. I swear I be feeling like James off good times like every time that nigga got 5 steps ahead something will knock his ass back 10 steps. It's like if it ain't one thing it's another," Rell told him.

"I feel you, bro my advice to you is to let this out and let it go. As much as you say you love Desire then I think you need to tell her. You don't gotta tell aunt Debra just keep this between you and ya wife," he told him.

Rell thought on it for a second he knew that's probably what he needed to do in order to let this go completely.

"Ight man you right and thanks," Rell told him.

"No problem bro now go get some rest," he told Rell.

"Ight goodnight bro," Rell said and ended the call.

"Baby are you ok?" Desire asked when she walked in the kitchen.

Rell jumped when he heard her voice "sorry baby I didn't mean to scare you what's wrong" she asked.

"Oh, you good bae and nothing just had to make a quick phone call," he told her.

"At almost 3 in the am? What kinda call you made?" she asked suspiciously.

Rell knew he wasn't going to get her off his back that easy.

"I called Tyquan bae now come on let's go back to sleep," he told her.

Desire looked him directly in the eyes "Terrell what's going on?" she asked seriously.

He started to fumble with the ends of his braids and desire knew something was wrong.

"Baby talk to me I'm right here I hate when you keep stuff in," she told him.

Rell went into the living room and sat down on the couch and Desire followed.

"The nightmares started again," Rell told her.

Desire rubbed his shoulder Rell had been having nightmares since they been together, but she thought that was just something he went through she never thought anything of it.

"Ok what was it about this time?" she asked.

"Diane it's always been about her or either Terrence," he told her.

"What happened in the dream?" she asked.

"I'm sitting in the corner and she's kicking and stomping me but I can't move and then all I hear is laughter and I look and I see Terrence laughing and pointing and then it will skip to a different scene like the shit keeps eatin' at me and I don't know why," Rell told her.

Desire held his hand she felt so bad he told her a couple times before about how his mom use to beat on him but she never knew it was that bad.

"Baby what happened next?" Des asked.

Rell pulled away from her and put his face in his hands she rubbed his back trying to console him but her heart broke into pieces when he looked at her as tears fell from his eyes.

"Oh, my god Terrell what's wrong baby? Please talk to me please you can't hold this in any longer," she told him.

Rell hesitated before speaking.

"Ma mom ... ma mom use to touch me," he told her.

"She molested you?" she asked.

"That too?" he told her.

Desire eyes grew big. "Rell she raped you?" she asked.

"Some nights she would just touch me, but other nights she would force herself on me," he said.

Desire shook her head in disbelief she couldn't believe people like Diane existed. Now she knew why he was so over protective about TJ and who they left him with and why he never wanted him to meet his mother.

"How long did it go on for?" Des asked.

Although she didn't want to pressure Rell to tell her anything she knew if he wanted to let this go that he needed to talk about it.

"I was 14 when it started. She would come in the bathroom when I was in the shower or when I was sleep at night she would get into bed with me. Sometimes when we went to supermarkets and I would go to the bathroom she would come in there and get on her knees and give me head or wake me up with it," Rell told her.

Desire couldn't believe the stuff she was hearing after all these years stuff was finally adding up. She now knew why Rell didn't like her giving him morning head or when she got on her knees to do it. Rell was scarred and she didn't know if she was gone be able to help him get over this.

"Rell baby how did you go so many years with this without talking to anyone or telling on her? That is why it keeps eating at you because you didn't let go nor did you forgive her for the things she's done," Desire said.

"Man, I don't want nobody to know that ma mom used to fuck me. What type of shit is that to tell somebody? Nah I ain't wanna go through that," he told her.

"Terrell there are plenty of people who went through the same exact thing so you are not alone in this," she told him.

"Des I'm good I don't need to talk to no one. Look how long it took me to tell you," Rell said.

"So, what about your dad? What did he do?" she asked.

"I'm tired and I just wanna go back to sleep," Rell told her.

Desire didn't pressure him she just followed him back to the bedroom. They got back into bed and laid down in the dark until they fell asleep.

ell woke up the next morning craving yesterday's dinner. He rolled out of bed and headed to the kitchen. He washed his hands and took out the food. While heating himself up a big plate Rell looked down at his dick bulging through his sweats.

"Yea, I think it's time to wake Des up to," he said with a laugh.

He wanted to forget about everything he told Desire yesterday. He had a life to live and he couldn't let his past bring him down. Rell made sure he warmed his food up twice before heading back to the room. TJ was still sound asleep and that made Rell happy because he planned on getting some morning dessert from Desire and he wanted no interruptions.

Sitting on the bed and placing his glass of juice on the stand Rell dug into his food like he hadn't ate in days. With each forkful, he scraped the plate. Desire tried to ignore it but it seem like he was trying to wake her up.

"Rell what do you want?" she asked in a groggy voice.

Rell smirked. "Nothing why you ask that?" Rell said.

"Because you're constantly making noises. I'm up now so what do you want?" Des asked.

Rell put his plate on the stand and rolled over on des while giving her morning kisses.

"Rell move, ya breath stank and get ya heavy ass off me my stomach is still sensitive," Desire told him.

Rell laughed. "Shut up, I'm not heavy and you gone give me some?" he asked.

"Give you what I just opened my eyes," Desire said.

Rell got up and shut the bedroom door and took off his clothes.

"Rell it is eight in the morning are you serious?"

"Hell, yea do you see this morning wood?" Rell said while holding his dick.

Desire rolled her eyes. "You like that every morning," Desire said.

"I know and that's why you be sore every morning," Rell shot back and got on top of her.

Rell sucked and licked on Desires neck. Her nipples got hard and her pussy started to thump

"Mmmm," Des moaned.

"See I knew you wanted dis dick," Rell said as he opened desire's legs and kissed her clit.

Des wrapped her legs around his neck and pushed his head down.

"You better stop playing with me," she said and Rell went to work on her pussy.

He teased her clit and sucked on it making her pull on his hair harder. Rell parted her pussy lips and began moving his tongue up and down making sure to catch all her juices as they flowed out.

"Ooh my god Rell," Desire screamed out.

He pushed her legs all the way back.

"Rell what are you doing my legs can't go that far back anymore," Desire panted.

Rell didn't respond his tongue met her ass and desire needed no explanation she was just in shock because Rell never did that and she never wanted him to but she regretted that because it felt so good. After cumin' almost 3 times Desire was weak, but Rell didn't care he held her legs open wide and slide his dick inside her as she gasped and tried to push him back a little but he grabbed her hands and put all his weight down while holding them back. His dick was deep in her stomach.

"Oooh, ooo, shit, oh god!" she moaned.

Rell was digging her out with no hesitation.

"Mmmm," Rell moaned and Desire came instantly.

That always made her cum fast and he never understood why. Rell started going faster and started slamming down on top of Des.

"Ooh fuck!" Desire screamed out.

"Shhh," Rell told her and put his hand over her mouth.

Desire was gripping on the sheets as Rell pounded away. All you heard was a smacking sound echoing through the house. It was too much for Desire she couldn't handle it. As soon as she was about to tap out Rell held onto her tight and came.

"Urggghhhh shit," he moaned as he came all inside of Desire and between her thighs.

Desire was too weak to move so she just laid there for a while and so did Rell. She looked over at the clock and it was 9:50 am.

She looked over at Rell. "Get up and get ya dishes out of here. I'm going back to sleep and make sure to give TJ some Tylenol when he wakes up my baby is catching a little cold," Des said

She turned over and did exactly what she said she was going to do. Rell got up and went into the bathroom to shower. He had a few things to do so he brushed his teeth and took a quick shower. After getting out he looked in the mirror.

"Damn I need my hair redone," he said to his self.

He wrapped the towel around his waist and walked in the bedroom.

"Des! Des!" he called out to her.

"What, Rell what?" She asked.

"Can you redo my braids this shit looking nappy?"

Desire sat up. "Rell you can't be serious?" she asked.

"Yea bae I got some shit to do today and you know I don't like going out looking any kind of way," he told her.

Desire blew and threw the covers back. She stormed into the bathroom to get the comb and grease.

"Get those damn dishes out of my room," she snapped when she walked back into the room.

Rell did what she told him he did not wanna hear anymore of her bitching this morning. He came back into the bedroom and put on his boxers and sweats.

"You ready?" he asked.

Desire didn't say anything she just waved him over. Rell sat between her legs on the bed and turned on the TV. Desire combed out his braids and then greased his hair real good.

"You need your hair washed," she told him.

"You gone wash it for me?" he asked.

"Yea maybe tomorrow I just wanna rest today. I'm tired I've been busy since we moved here," Desire said.

She parted his hair and began to braid each part in neat corn rows straight back. After she was done Rell finished getting dress by this time TJ woke up. So Rell fed him breakfast gave him some Tylenol and got him dress.

"Oh, so you taking him with you today?" Des asked.

"Yea but then I'ma drop him off at my mom's because I gotta go pick up this money from Philly and you know I don't want him around when I'm handling my business," Rell said.

"Ok well you be safe and I'll talk to you later," Des said and then gave him a big kiss.

"Ok I love you," she said

"I love you too," Rell told her before leaving out.

Week Later. . .

*A*It had been almost a week since Desire heard from Rell. She was worried sick because this wasn't like him. She kept calling his phone but it went straight to voicemail. She reached out to Mark but he hadn't heard from Rell either.

"This isn't like him," Desire said.

"Desire don't worry I filed a missing person's report everything will be fine," Robert told her.

"You don't understand this isn't like Rell something's wrong," Desire said.

Robert didn't speak on it he didn't want to worry desire any more than she already was. He went out of the room and made a phone call after about 5 minutes he came back.

"Look Desire I have to make a quick run I'll be back ok," Robert told her and then headed out.

Desire sat down on the couch and tried to call Rell again, but she still had no luck. Around 9pm that night Desire's phone rang. She quickly picked it up hoping it was Rell.

"Hello?" she answered quickly.

"DESIRE THEY FOUND HIM!" Debra screamed through the phone.

Desire jumped up "Oh my god where? Please tell me he's ok?" she asked.

Debra paused before speaking. "Desire baby they found his body, he's dead," Debra told her.

"NOOOOO!" Desire screamed as she dropped the phone.

The entire world came crashing down on her at once. Her best friend, her soul mate, the only man she ever loved had just been found dead. She felt as though her life was over. Tears ran down her face as she hugged herself. Apart of her was gone and she didn't know what to do. Desire laid down and closed her eyes she couldn't wait for this dream to be over.

ell's funeral was just days away desire was barely eating or sleeping. She didn't have the strength to handle the funeral arrangements so Debra and Mattie did it for her.

"Desire you have to get up and eat something," said Robert.

"I'm fine please just leave me alone," she told him.

Robert didn't bother her he just left out of the room. TJ came in the room and climbed on the bed

"Mommy where Daddy go?" TJ asked.

Desire broke down crying. She didn't know how to explain Rell's death to TJ. She had been telling him that daddy went away. She wiped her face and looked at him

"Remember when I told you that my mom was an angel in the sky watching over me?" Desire asked him.

"Yea," said TJ.

"Well now daddy is an angel in the sky watching over you," she told him.

TJ smiled. "I go with daddy to?" he asked.

"No baby you can't go with daddy, but I want you to know that daddy loved you very much and he wants you to be strong ok," Desire said.

"Ok mommy," TJ said as he laid beside her.

Desire held him tight as she cried hard; she wasn't prepared for this ride she was about to go on. She heard a knock on her bedroom door she looked up and saw Debra.

"Hey are you ok?" she asked.

"I will never be ok," Des said to her.

"Sweetie you are going to be fine. Rell wants you to stay strong he wouldn't want you to stress like this," Debra told her.

"How the hell would you know that? Look please just stop while your ahead I don't want to talk right now," Desire said.

Debra saw the hurt in Desire. She couldn't believe she actually played a part in everything, she felt so guilty. She went back out into the living room where Robert sat.

"How is she doing?" Robert asked.

"Not good at all," Debra responded.

Robert didn't seem bothered by the fact that Rell was dead and Debra noticed all of it.

"She will be ok. Desire is a strong girl she's been through worse," said Robert.

Debra shook her head she didn't understand how someone could be so cold during a time like this.

"She just needs us to be by her side right now," Debra said.

"No, I have some important business to handle so this is going to have to wait, but I'm sure you can hold things down," Robert said as he got up.

"What's the rush? I mean this is family business Rell was her husband," Debra said.

"Her soon to be husband. I mean if you ask me this may be good for Desire because if it wasn't for Rell then she wouldn't have went through half the shit she did go through," Robert stated.

Debra was not feeling the way he was bad talking Rell so she stood up.

"Listen here, Robert you will not down talk my son like that. If you had anything against him you should have said it while he was still here on this earth, but you rather bitch up when he's around and talk shit when he's not around.

Just know you will reap what you sow and that's facts," Debra said as she went over to the door and opened it.

Robert knew that was his cue to leave.

For the next couple of days Desire could barely sleep. Knowing that Rell's funeral was getting near killed her inside.

"TJ come here why did you spill this juice and not pick it up?" Desire asked.

TJ came running from the back room. "Sorry mommy I clean it," TJ told her.

"No, I'll clean it but next time you spill something you betta make sure you pick it up or tell me," she told him.

TJ ran back to his room without even responding to Desire. As she was cleaning up the juice she found herself crying.

"Rell baby I can't do this without you," she said out loud.

Desire finished cleaning up the juice and then went to her room. She picked up her cell and called Debra. She got no answer. Desire realized that Debra would barely answer her calls, but she would always come by to see what she needed. Her uncle Robert ignored all her calls and texts and she felt betrayed because she thought he would be there for her in her time of need. She heard a knock at the door and went to answer it.

"What up bro," she greeted him.

"Hey sis how you holding up?" he asked as he walked in.

"To be totally honest I'm going through it. This shit is hard like, I never thought I would lose him and now that he's gone I feel like the whole fuckin' world is on ma shoulders," Desire said.

Mark sat down on the couch and Desire followed.

"Yea I feel you this shit ain't easy to take in at all," he told her.

"Did he say anything about anyone bothering him? I mean I knew Rell could protect his self but did he mention anyone," Desire asked.

Mark was getting uncomfortable and desire could tell.

"Look Desire, I don't know anything but just hit me up if you need anything I just came by to check on you," he said as he got up.

"Wait what's going on Mark? I mean damn if you know something you need to tell me," she asked.

Mark shook his head. "Take care sis," Mark told her as he walked out.

Desire knew something was up she didn't want to believe the thought she was thinking but she couldn't help herself. She got up from the couch and went to TJ's room.

"It's time for bed," she told him.

"No mommy," TJ whined.

Desire put him in bed and tucked him in "Look TJ it's time for bed don't give me that no shit, not tonight," Des said sternly.

TJ saw that Desire was not playing and he got with the program quick.

"Night, night mommy" said TJ.

"Good night," Des said back.

She turned his light off and then turned on his night light. She went into her bedroom and sat on the bed. Tomorrow was the day that the love of her life was going to be put 6 feet under and she didn't know how she was going to take it. Desire laid down and cried herself to sleep she just wanted this nightmare to end.

The next morning Desire barely had any energy she didn't want to get out of bed but she did. She fed TJ and got his washed up and dressed. He looked so handsome in his black suit. Terrell had one just like it they both wore it once and that was for a special occasion.

"Ok now I want you to stay in here while mommy gets dressed ok," Desire said.

"Ok mommy," said TJ.

Desire went into the bedroom to get dressed. She put on her grey dress pants and her black tank top. After putting lotion on her arms, she put on her jacket that matched her pants. Desire looked in the mirror and combed out her wrap she wasn't worried about looking her best so she only put on

134

some chap stick. Desire slid on her flats and she was good to go.

"Ok TJ are you ready?" Desire called out.

"Yes, mommy we go see daddy now?" asked TJ.

"Yes, baby for the last time," Desire told him.

She put on his jacket and grabbed her car keys. When she opened the door, she was shocked to see who was standing on the other side. She grabbed TJ and pulled her gun out of her purse

"Chill ma I'm not on no dumb shit I'm just tryna figure out what the fuck is going on?" Terrence told her.

"Nigga you always on some dumb shit now what the fuck do you want?" she said without taking the gun off him.

"I came to talk to you," he told her.

"What the fuck do you wanna talk about huh? How you killed my husband?" Desire snapped.

Terrence looked confused "First of all, I don't give a fuck about that gun in your hand because I'm already a dead man walking. Secondly, I don't know what you talking about but I ain't seen or heard from Terrell in a couple and then I see in the newspaper that he's dead. So, I came to see what the hell is going on and to talk about Trina," he told her.

"So, you ain't have shit to do with this?" Desire asked.

"Nah not even," he told her.

"I'm on my way to his funeral now," Desire told him.

Terrence stared at her for a minute before he spoke.

"Listen here baby girl I might be a nasty nigga and I know I might be the last one you trust but my brother ain't dead I would've felt it," said Terrence.

Desire didn't know what he was talking about all she knew was that Terrell was dead and now Terrence was coming out of the wood works. She knew someone was lying to her but she didn't know who and she didn't know why.

"What do you mean?" she asked.

"I would've felt if anything happened to him. Look I don't know what's going on around here but all I know is that I need to find Trina and when I do I'm going to kill her," said Terrence.

"Look I don't know if Trina's dead or alive and to keep it real I really don't give a fuck whether she is or not. To be honest I want no parts of any of you," Desire said.

Terrence knew that he wasn't going to get anything out of desire and he couldn't blame her. He couldn't expect her to trust him all he wanted to know was where he could find Trina.

"It seems like ya mind is made up, but one more thing before I go Terrell isn't dead somebody is lying to you," he told her and then walked off.

Desire mind was in a million places right now. She put her gun away and then grabbed TJ. She locked up the house and went to put TJ in the car. Before she could pull off she got a call from Debra

"Hello?" Desire answered.

"Desire it won't be a funeral."

Debra blurted out.

"Excuse me what the fuck do you mean it won't be a damn funeral? Well what will it be?" Desire snapped.

"It's just to keep you and TJ out of harm's way," Debra told her.

Desire felt her body get hot she couldn't even speak because her mouth was so dry. She ended the call and sped off. Desire made it to Debra's house in less than 20 minutes. She got out and grabbed TJ. She ran up to her door and banged and kicked it. As soon as Debra opened it Desire hit her with a 2 banger.

"Bitch what the fuck is going on?" Desire huffed.

Debra slowly got up off the floor and Desire hit her again.

"No bitch stay down until I tell you to get up. It's some sneaky shit going on and I wanna know wassup," Desire barked.

Debra saw the seriousness in Desire face which hurt her heart. She never thought it would come to this but her being involved with everything that had happened made her the main target.

"Desire I'm sorry sweetie I know this all looks bad, but it's not what you think," Debra pleaded.

TJ grabbed Desires leg and she looked down at him.

"Bitch if it wasn't for my son I would've mopped the floor with your ass. If I even think you up to something else I'm coming back here and next time TJ won't be with me," Desire warned and then she walked out.

"I'm sorry you had to see that baby, but sometimes the ones close to you are the ones that hurts you the most," Desire told him as she put him in the car.

She was on her way back home when she saw fire trucks speeding past her.

"Lord no!" she said out loud.

Desire raced home and she couldn't believe what she saw. Her house was on fire.

"THIS IS BULLSHIT I WAS ONLY GONE FOR A FEW MINUTES!" she screamed as she got out.

She ran up to one of the fire men "Excuse me, what happened?" she asked.

"It was an electrical fire ma'am," said the firemen.

Desire was confused she had only been gone for a few minutes she didn't believe any of that. She looked over and saw her Uncle Robert talking to another fireman.

"This is impossible somebody is trying to make me suffer," she told him.

The firemen shook his head "I'm sorry ma'am I'm just doing my job. Is there anyone you can stay with because the house is damaged pretty badly," he told her.

Desire shook her head no and walked away and headed towards where her uncle was standing.

"What the hell happened?" she asked Robert.

"When I pulled up I saw that your house was on fire. I couldn't do anything but call 911; once they got here and did their job I was informed that this was an electrical fire," Robert explained.

None of this made any sense. Desire was so ready to go on a killing spree. She wanted to kill everyone who she thought might have betrayed her.

"This is bullshit," Desire said.

She went back to her car and pulled off.

*T*errence searched all over for Trina but he always came up empty handed. He wasn't going to give up just yet though. Terrence knocked 3 times before he answered the door.

"Ahhhh, I knew I would see you sooner or later come in," said Donnie.

Terrence walked into his house. "Well sit down make yourself at home," Donnie told him.

"Nah I'm straight I only came here for one thing and one thing only," said Terrence.

"What's that?" he asked.

"Tell me where Trina is," said Terrence.

Donnie shook his head and smiled "Now why would I do such a thing?" he asked.

Terrence pulled out a blade.

"I'm pretty sure you know how I get down since you did a background check on me. So, listen up muthafucker ya daughter is around here spreading AIDS and shit, and I'ma be the one to stop her. So, either you tell me where she is or you just tell me where the fuck she is," Terrence barked.

Donnie gave Terrence a serious look "What are you talking about?" he asked.

"You heard what I said ma nigga. If you took care of her rather than stickin' ya dick up in her every chance you got she might of turned out decent and hell you was fucking her too so I'm pretty sure she done gave it to you as well," said Terrence.

Donnie rolled over to his bar and got a drink "What happened to you anyway?" he asked.

"That little bitch Terrell did this to me. I'm glad that fuckers' dead I hope he's rotting in hell," Donnie spat.

Terrence didn't like the way he was talking. He didn't care if him and Rell didn't like each other or not he was tired of Donnie running his mouth about him.

"Yo where is Trina?" he asked again.

"She's in some hospital not sure which one," Donnie said as he waved him off.

"Good, see now that wasn't so hard, but check this you been getting real slick out the mouth lately so while I'm here I might as well finish you off," said Terrence.

He caught Donnie by surprise when he rushed him and grabbed his head and pulled it back.

"You just got yourself a one-way ticket to hell nigga," Terrence whispered before slicing his throat.

Donnie grabbed his neck as his eyes nearly popped out. Terrence headed for the door, but turned around when he heard a gurgling sound coming from Donnie. He thought about what Trina had done and to think that Donnie didn't have a care in a world for his daughter's actions burned him up inside.

"It's payback time," Terrence said as he went over to Donnie's bar and started knocking the liquor over and smashing bottles on the floor. He took a lighter out of his pocket and lit Donnie's shirt on fire and rolled him over to the bar

"Burn bitch burn," Terrence laughed as he ran out of the house.

He felt like his missions was almost accomplished, but he needed to make one more visit and that was to see Diane. He wanted her to know that he would no longer be her puppet not now not ever.

*O*ver the next 3 weeks Desire and TJ had been living out of a hotel. She was still stressed but it seemed as though she was dealing with it a lot better. Whenever she left her hotel room she would smell a strong scent of Terrell's cologne she knew that just meant his presence was watching over her at all times. Her cell phone went off and to her surprise it was Debra

"What da fuck do you want?" she asked with attitude.

"Desire I know you don't want to talk to me, but I found a place for you and TJ. I think you guys will love it," Debra said excitedly.

"No, me and TJ is fine we don't need or want any of your help," Desire told her.

"Desire please, I know I screwed up, but I have a good reason for all of this," Debra pleaded.

"Why do I feel like you and my uncle had something to do with my husband's death?" Desire finally said.

Debra was silent for a moment.

"Desire please, I know you hate me but I want you and TJ to have a home. It's in Delaware and I know you don't want to move back to Jersey but this place is beautiful Desire please check it out please," Debra begged.

Desire thought about it for a minute she was tired of her and her son living out of a hotel room so she decided that she would at least check the house out.

"Fine, ill check it out, but if there's any bullshit involved I'm kickin' ya shit in again," she told her.

"Great, I'll text you the address," Debra said and then ended the call.

No sooner than 5 minutes Debra text her the address.

Desire looked at TJ "You wanna go for a ride lil man?" she asked him.

He smiled and nodded his head and off they went.

I t took Terrence almost 2 hours to find out what hospital Trina was in but he finally found it. He pulled up to the Vineland new jersey hospital and got out. He walked in and went to the front desk

"I'm here to see Trina Boyd. I'm her boyfriend," he told the lady.

"Take one of the visitor's passes and she's in room 225," she told him.

He couldn't believe it was that easy. He took the elevator to the second floor and got off. He walked down to the end of the hall and made a right

"Ahhh 225," he said with a smile.

He opened the door slowly and walked in quietly. Trina had her eyes closed he stood there and starred at her for a while apart of him wanted to kill her but then apart of him wanted to make sure she suffered. Terrence took out his blade and tapped her on the thigh. Trina opened her eyes and smiled.

"Hey baby, what you are doing here?" she asked.

Terrence looked at her like she was a silly rabbit he couldn't believe she had the audacity to call him baby.

"Bitch don't call me baby and I'm here for payback," he told her.

Trina winced in pain as she sat up "Payback for what?" she asked confused.

"Payback for me, Briana, and my unborn child," he told her.

Trina started to get mad. "You mean you're here because of that bitch?" she spat.

Terrence grabbed her by her throat.

"That bitch your referring to was pregnant with my baby and she told me the truth about your scandalous ass. My life is over because of you," Terrence said as he tightened his grip around her neck.

Trina clawed at him trying to get him off but he wouldn't let go.

"I...I'm. So...sorry," Trina said as she gasped for air.

"Bitch you ain't sorry. You don't give a fuck about nobody but yourself. You one evil bitch and it took me this long to find out," he said as he let her go.

Trina grabbed her neck and rubbed it as she watched Terrence pace back and forth.

"You ain't shit bitch and I can't wait until karma gets you. I wana be there when you take your last breath because sooner or later somebody is gonna off your ass," he told her.

Trina managed to crack a smile "You know how long I've been doing this? Since I was 15 years old muthafucker, and ain't nobody stopped me yet. I just got 3 bullets to the stomach not too long ago and I'm still here. I'm unstoppable and you or anyone else can't stop me. I'm TRINA THE HBIC PUSSY!" she yelled.

Terrence had finally had enough his plans had change from killing her to just letting her know how messed up she was but the joy in her voice when she that to him push a button that she shouldn't have pushed. Terrence walked over to her and grabbed her by her throat again this time he put all his strength into it. He threw the sheets off her and pulled up her hospital gown.

"I'm going to make sure you suffer for the rest of your fucked-up life. This is for me and everyone else you gave this poison to," he said as he took his blade and stabbed her numerous times in her vagina.

Trina tried to scream but his grip on her throat wouldn't let her. Her body began to shake as her eyes rolled in the back of her head. Terrence stopped after he seen that she had enough

"I want you to remember this every time you think about doing something fucked up. Remember what goes around comes right back the fuck around," said Terrence as he put his blade away.

He washed his hands and wiped down everything he touched. He threw up the peace sign at a bleeding Trina and left out. He took the stairs instead of the elevator so he wouldn't be seen. Once he was outside he felt a relief

"I did that for us baby girl," he said as he looked up to the sky.

36

"This is beautiful TJ look at this," Desire said once she entered the house.

She couldn't believe how it already felt like home. Everything was fully furnished and it was just how she liked. It was a 4-bedroom house with a full backyard, bathrooms a full basement and a beautiful living room and kitchen.

"TJ look this must be your room it's amazing!" she said excitedly as her and TJ jumped up and down.

TJ ran around the room and started getting out toys. Desire was amazed she didn't feel nervous anymore she felt safe and she didn't know why. Desire went to check out the other rooms which was a guess room and when she tried to open the door to the next room she couldn't because it was locked.

"What the hell?" she said out loud.

"Oooo, mommy!" TJ said as he came out the room.

"Oh, sorry sweetie mommy just wanted to know why this damn door is locked," Desire said.

TJ shrugged his shoulders and ran back into his room to play with the toys. She checked out the bathroom.

"Oh, my gosh this is beautiful," she screamed.

It was burgundy and cream through the whole bathroom. The shower curtains had different cartoon characters on it and so did the matching rug. Desire was all smiles. She ran out of the bathroom and into the living room.

"Uhhhh, I am in heaven right now Rell baby I wish you were here to see this," she said.

The living room was Smokey black, white, and grey all over. The carpet was so soft Desire took her shoes off and sighed as her feet sunk deep into it. It was a sectional black and grey couch that wrapped around nearly half of the living room. There was an 80inch sharp class full HD TV. Desire turned the TV on and put on some music. She was home and she didn't plan on leaving. She walked into the kitchen and melted. Desire loved to cook so seeing how big the kitchen was made her happy. The kitchen was painted all white with gold trimmings everywhere; everything coordinated so well with the colors. Her dining room and kitchen were connected and that's just how she liked it. Desire couldn't help but to look out the sliding door that showed her backyard.

"TJ COME HERE!" she screamed. TJ came running full speed out of the room and into the kitchen.

"Look at the backyard," she told him.

TJ jumped up in joy when he saw the playground.

"Mommy I want go play," he said as he wiggled.

"Ok baby lets go," she told him and they both ran outside.

They played on the swings together and slid down the sliding board. They ran after each other and rolled on the ground in the snow.

"Mommy I'm happy," TJ told her.

"I'm happy too baby. Welcome to your new home," Desire told them.

"Yay! Now I'm hungry," TJ said.

Desire started laughing.

"Ok, let's see if we can find something good to eat," Desire said as she picked him up and went back into the house.

When she got back inside the kitchen she smelled Rell's cologne. She put TJ down and started looking all around the house but no one was there. She thought she was going crazy. Desire went back into the kitchen and opened the fridge and it was fully loaded.

"TJ, we bouta go ham baby boy," Desire told him.

She took out some hamburgers and some potatoes.

"Hamburgers and homemade French fries ok lil man?" she asked.

"Ok mommy," TJ said as he walked into the living room.

Desire started peeling the potatoes and cutting them up. She took out her cell and called Debra

"Oh, my god I just wanted to say thank you. I love it and when can I speak to the previous owner about buying this house because I love it," Desire said excitedly.

"Baby the house is yours. It's a gift from me, I'm sorry about everything that went on. I know Rell's death was hard for you and I want you and TJ to be well taken care of. You don't need to thank me this is all for you two" Debra told her.

"Wow I don't know what to say Debra," desire said lost for words.

"You've said enough as long as you're happy that's all that matters," she told her.

"Thank you I appreciate that. Well let me get back to cooking for your greedy grandson I'll talk to you later," Desire said.

"Ok baby talk to you soon," Debra said and ended the call.

Desire couldn't stop smiling even though Rell was gone she was still blessed; he gave her a wonderful son and love that can never be broken. She finished up cooking and her and TJ chowed down

"Mommy good," TJ said with a full mouth.

"I see and thank you I'm glad you like it," Des told him.

They ate and talked about SpongeBob. Desire cleaned up and then gave TJ a bath. By the time she got done it was going on 10:30pm.

"Welp, it's a Friday night I might as well relax," she said to herself.

She went into the master bedroom and fell in love all over again. The king-sized bed the plush carpet was everything to her. Desire looked in the closet and dresser and it already had clothes in it.

"Debra, you really out did yourself this time. I kinda feel bad for putting hands on you," Desire said.

She took out some pajama shorts and a tank top. Desire went in the bathroom and turned on the shower. Her vanilla bean body was already there. She shook her head impressed by all that Debra had done. She was feeling kind of bad for punching her in the face, but she had to know that was going to be the consequences because of her actions. After washing up desire rinsed off and got out. She dried off and went into the bedroom. Desire lotion her whole body and then put on her clothes. She sat down on the bed and turned on the TV.

"Lord thank you," she said as she laid back and relaxed.

Desire watched 2 movies and finally felt herself getting tired. She drifted off to sleep and seen herself dreaming of Rell again. She jumped up out of her sleep. Desire felt her panties and they were wet and once again she smelled Rell's cologne. That dream had her hot and bothered. Finally getting herself together desire laid back down and it seemed as though her dream continued.

A month later, Desire was succeeding in her college
classes. She was thinking about opening up a
restaurant since she loved to cook, but she wasn't sure yet.
Desire only had 1 more year and then she would be
graduating she was so proud of herself.

"TJ mommy is cooking tacos tonight and I'm baking
chocolate chip cookies," she told him.

"Yayyyyy cookies, cookies, cookies," TJ cheered.

Desire laughed and went into the kitchen. She put the
meat on and let it cook. While she was chopping up the sides
she heard the doorbell ring. She got up and went to the door.

"Aye what up watchu doing here?" she asked.

Desire was so happy to see him she felt like since Rell's death that everyone betrayed her.

"You know I couldn't stay away from baby sis too long. Debra told me where you lived so I had to come stop by and see how you was making out. I know this last month or so has been hard for you," he told her.

"Come on in and yea it has but I'm getting through it," she told him.

TJ ran up to Mark and he picked him up and spun him around.

"Wassup nephew I missed you," Mark told him.

"Me too," TJ said.

"You been being good," he asked.

"Yes," said TJ.

"Good, that's what I like to hear," Mark told him as he dug in his pocket and pulled out a 50-dollar bill and handed it to TJ.

"Are you crazy? What do a 2-year-old need with that kind of money?" Desire asked him.

"You never know he might wanna by some juice for the ladies," Mark said with a laugh.

"You are too much," Desire said as she went back into the kitchen.

Desire finished up cooking and gave Mark a plate.

"Thanks Des. So, I'ma get out of here but I'ma hit you up tomorrow I promise and you let me know if you need anything," he told her.

"Ok bro and thanks," Des told him.

Mark nodded his head as he took a big bite of his taco. He wiped his hands on his jeans and left out. Desire laughed at how greedy he was. She put TJ in a chair at the table and gave him his food. Before she could sit down and eat she heard a knock at the door.

"Damn who the hell is it," she huffed.

"RJ," he said from the other side of the door.

The voice sounded very familiar, but she didn't know anyone by the name RJ. When she opened the door, she saw a man standing there

"Can I help you?" she asked.

"Yea 1 have some very important information for you can I please come in?" he said.

"We can speak right here," she told him.

"I think it would be best if I came in," he responded.

Desire didn't have a bad feeling from this RJ guy so she let him in. When he came in there was another man behind him, but she couldn't get a good look at him because of the hoodie he had on.

"Ok so what is this about?" she asked.

"Robert Boyd also known as Slim he was an ex drug addict and he is also the half-brother of James Boyd and Donnie Johnson," RJ explained.

Desire was lost for words "You two need to talk before I go any further," RJ told her.

He moved to the side so Desire could see who he was referring to. When the guy took his hood off her mouth dropped open.

"This can't be real," she said to herself.

He was still so very handsome to her even with the unhealed wounds. Desire walked up to him slowly and touched his face

"I thought you were dead," she told him. He kissed her hand.

"I told you I will never leave you and TJ," Rell responded.

Terrence sat at the visitors table waiting for Diane to come out. He had a nervous feeling in his stomach, but he tried to shake it before she got there. The buzzer went off and in walked the inmates. Terrence sat in awe when he seen a lot of younger girls coming out. They couldn't have been no older than 16 because they were coming out rushing to hug who he thought may have been their mothers. Finally, Diane walked out her long curly hair had been freshly braided in neat cornrows going straight back. The time she spent in there was doing her some justice because she gained a few pounds and she was getting thicker.

"Hey baby," she greeted him with a hug, but Terrence didn't hug her back.

"Wassup Diane?" he greeted her dryly she sensed some tension so she sat down slowly.

"What's going on?" she asked.

Terrence put his hands in his pockets before he spoke.

"Look, I came to tell you that I ain't fuckin' with you no more. I'm tired of being ya puppet all this beef shit is because of you and I'm done," he told her.

Diane gave him a cold look "You think you just gone walk in here and tell me you done with me bitch nigga I own you!" Diane told him.

Terrence shook his head in disgust "You know for a long time I believed everything you said. You told me never to trust no woman but you, you told me that my brother hated me because you liked me better, you told me the things my dad did to me was normal, but all of that was BULLSHIT!" Terrence snapped.

"Listen here muthafucka!" Diane said but Terrence cut her off.

"No, you listen bitch I took a lot of shit from you and I did a lot of shit for you. I started beef with my brother because you said so and I pushed away every woman I came in contact with because you said so, but now I'm done fuck you and the ground you walk on. I'm changing all the contact information you have for me and I never want to see or hear from you again. It's because of you I'm a fucked up individual, it's because of you me and my brothers don't like each other, it's because of you the only girl who actually loved me for me is dead, and last but not least it's because of you that I will never get the chance to be a father," Terrence told her.

He got up, and Diane grabbed his arm. He snatched away and looked at her as if she was a germ.

"This isn't over Terrence," Diane yelled after him.

"I know it's not, but bitch I guarantee you won't win this war," he said as he chucked up the deuces and walked out.

Diane waited until Terrence left and asked could she make a phone call she was burning up inside. When the person on the other end picked up she spoke in code.

"Yea it's about that time you came back and marked ya territory for the last time," She told them and then ended the call.

After the visit, Terrence felt like a weight had been lifted off him. Before he went home he decided to get something to eat and do a little shopping. So, he stopped by one of the seafood spots in Philly and got him a platter. After getting his food, he stopped by one of his favorite clothing spots and pick up a few things. Terrence was going to enjoy life while he was still alive. He figured he deal with his past demons another time. He shopped for a little bit more and then realized he had his food in the car.

"Damn," he said to himself as he headed back to his car.

He put the bags in the trunk and closed it. He got in the car and checked his cell. Terrence had a few missed calls but didn't bother to look at them. He wanted to get home as soon as possible. Terrence pulled into his driveway and got out and went to open his door. When he unlocked it, and walked in he saw Tyshawn sitting on his couch with a machete beside him.

"Welcome home son," Tyshawn said with a smirk.

Terrence dropped his food and pulled out his gun.

"The fuck you doing here nigga?" he asked.

"Now is that any way to greet the man who brought you into this world?" Tyshawn asked.

"Man fuck you it's because of you and that bitch ass Diane that I'ma fucked up individual now," he barked.

Tyshawn stood up which made Terrence back up he made sure he kept one foot outside just in case he needed to make a run for it.

"Shut the fuck up you pussy if you was half the man I am you would've killed Rell like your mother told you to, but no I had to come out and do it myself," Tyshawn stated.

Terrence looked at the machete and then at the man who use to be his father. Tyshawn seen where he was looking and smiled as he picked up the machete.

"You know I gotta mean ass aim right," he told him.

Terrence debated on whether he should run or not. He knew if he stayed there any longer that Tyshawn was going to kill him for not killing Rell but he also knew that if he run then that would make things far much worse. He shrugged his shoulders.

"Fuck it I knew my time would come someday but I ain't going out without a fight," Terrence said as he raised his gun and took the first shot.

Tyshawn moved and the bullet went past him and into the wall.

"My turn," said Tyshawn as he raised the machete.

Terrence tried to dart out of the house but he felt a piercing pain go through his back. Terrence instantly fell to the ground.

"You stupid son of a bitch! You should've just did what your mother asked of you," Tyshawn said as he pulled Terrence back in the house.

He threw the machete on the ground and pulled Terrence jeans off. He ripped his boxers clean off him and rammed his dick inside of him

"Ahhhhhh!" Terrence yelled as blood poured from his mouth.

"Shut the fuck up you should be used to this," Tyshawn barked.

He continued to ram his dick in and out of Terrence. Terrence tried to get away, but Tyshawn dug his nails inside of the open wound on his back.

"Arghhhhh! Please stop!" he stuttered.

All Tyshawn did was laugh as he dug his nails deeper into the wound and pounded Terrence until he released. He came all over Terrence's open wound and laughed as he screamed in pain.

"This should teach you to do as you're told. Now I'm gonna go handle that bitch Desire and that little bastard TJ," he spat as he stood up and pulled up his pants and grabbed his machete.

Terrence just laid there in pain. He had no clue if he was going to live or not, but he was just hoping and praying that Terrell was ready for the return of their father. He knew his brother wasn't dead. No matter what they had against each other they shared a special bond. Terrence could always feel when Terrell was going through something or if something happened to him. He knew that Terrell was still having nightmares of him and his mother and he knew if he could feel and know those things then Terrell could too. Terrence knew that Terrell wasn't dead.

"Desire stop crying I'm here now," Rell told her.

"How can you tell me to stop crying Terrell? I thought you were dead, I don't understand. I need to know what happened," Desire said.

"Remember when I left that day and I said I was going to Philly?" Rell asked.

Desire thought back to the last day she had saw Rell "Yea I remember," she told him.

"After I dropped TJ off at my mom's house I went and spoke to ya uncle about a few things and after I left I noticed I was being followed. I couldn't see who was in the truck because their windows was tinted. The next thing I knew I was getting rammed from behind. I mean they rammed the back of ma car so hard that ma head jerked back and hit the steering wheel when I came forward," Rell explained.

"So why did everyone say you were dead?" Desire asked.

Rell put TJ down and winced a little as he rubbed his side.

"Ma car went off the road and flipped three times because of the impact when I was hit from behind. When I came to I was being put in the ambulance that's all I remember," Rell told her.

"So, what happened after that?" she asked.

Rell nodded at RJ "That's where I come in at. After I saw what went down I followed the ambulance to see what hospital they were taking him to. I didn't visit him until after a few days," RJ told her.

"Wait a minute what do you mean after everything went down?" Desire asked him.

"I was following Rell, but it's not what you think. I was actually coming to talk to you and let you know that you were being played apparently, I didn't make it in time," he told her.

Desire still wasn't catching on and Rell knew it "Desire Robert been setting us up since day one. He's been in on this too and to make things worse he's not even a detective," Rell said.

"Wait all of this is confusing," Desire said.

"James, Robert, and Donnie are all half-brother's. Donnie was dating your mother Marie and got her pregnant with Trina after she had the baby she started dating James and that made Donnie livid. Not to mention a little while after that your mother got pregnant with you," RJ explained.

"Robert was a crack head at that time so he was doing anything for a hit. When Donnie told him, what was up and that he would give him money if he helped him handle something Robert was all ears," Rell chimed in.

"That's where Trina comes in at she was just the bait, but they all played a part in the fire," RJ told her.

Desire was lost for words. The more they talked the more everything made sense. Since day one Robert cared way too much and he knew too much, but the question was how? If he wasn't a detective how did he know everything? Desire started suspecting her uncle when he gave her the lock box that he claimed he never opened. She also knew something wasn't right when Mattie slipped up and called Robert Slim. Desire sat quietly she tried to let everything marinate in her brain. She thought back to the day that her uncle found out that Trina killed her parents. She found out that Donnie helped Trina get out of everything, but why didn't her uncle try to stop it? Desire thought about every time her uncle called to inform them that Terrence wasn't dead, but not once did he try to get him arrested. Her uncle knew so much, but not once did he try to get the charges on Trina and Terrence to stick.

"So how do you know all of this?" Desire asked.

"Because I'm his son my name is Robert Jr. you don't know about me because I'm pretty sure he told you I was killed, right? Well yea I was shot, but I didn't die" said RJ.

Desire stood up "THIS SHIT IS CRAZY!" she said loudly.

Rell told TJ to go in his bedroom "I know bae that's the same thing I said when I found out," Rell told her.

"So, who all knew you were alive?" she asked.

"Mark, Tyquan and my mother," Rell told her.

Desire felt terrible. Now she understood why Debra and Mark were acting funny.

"Rell I gotta tell you something," Desire said.

"You punched ma mom in the face I know she told me," Rell said with a chuckle.

"Baby I'm so sorry I thought she had something to do with everything," Des told him.

"I know bae like I said it's cool. Shit, when she told me that I knew you was ma true ride or die," Rell said.

Desire smiled she couldn't believe she had her baby back none of this seemed real.

"So where have you been this whole time and were you the one who got us this house?" Desire asked.

"Don't worry about that just know I've been closer than you think and yea I told my mother to get the money out ma bank account I had to make sure yawl was good especially after I heard about the fire," Rell told her.

Desire wanted to slap herself in the face if she would have put all the pieces together then she would have known that Rell was alive the entire time. She wondered why Debra called her about a house all of a sudden, but she never questioned it.

"So, what about you?" she said referring to RJ.

"One day I heard my dad and Donnie talking about the fire and I confronted ma dad about it which at the time that was the wrong thing to do because he was on that stuff. That same night he came in my room and shot me 4 times only 2 shots hit me," said RJ.

"So, what happened after that?" Des asked.

"My mother was the one who saved me. She rushed me to the hospital when she found me in my room. However, she did leave me after she found out I was ok, she told my father that I was dead and after I was healed enough I left the hospital and was on my own ever since," RJ explained.

Desire was relieved that she was finally getting the truth for once, but she was still unsure if she could trust RJ or not and she still wanted to know how her uncle acted as if he was a detective and he wasn't.

"How do I know if we can trust you or not?" Desire asked.

"Look, all I can say is just watch my actions because there's no way I can convince yawl that I'm not on no dumb shit," RJ told them.

Desire and Rell looked at each other, at this point and time actions was all they could rely on because they had been told so many lies and been screwed so many times. Desire noticed that Rell kept wincing in pain as they all talked.

"Baby what's wrong?" she asked.

"Something happened to Terrence because I can feel it," Rell said.

*A*few days passed since Rell has been back in the picture. RJ let out a lot more information to Desire and Rell. He also hip them to Robert and Tyshawn knowing each other. They all prepared for what was about to go down because this time instead of waiting for anyone to come to them they were going to pay Robert a visit.

"Damn, I guess it's one down and one more to go," Rell said as he read the morning newspaper.

"What are you talking about?" asked Des.

"Ex detective Donnie Johnson was killed in a house fire," Rell read out loud.

Desire shook her head she didn't feel bad one bit because of everything he had put her through. It seemed as though the ball was in their court because they were getting answers to all of their unanswered questions.

"Well on a more positive note I'm so glad you're back in our lives and it seems like you're healing up well," Desire said as she gave Rell a kiss.

"I'm glad to be back. I mean the whole time I was laying low I was praying that you and TJ was safe," Rell said.

"Well Terrence told me that you wasn't dead. He even said that he would have felt it is that true," Desire said.

"Yea it is, anyway I'm glad TJ won't be in the middle of all this damn drama. I swear to you I'll be glad when this shit is over," Rell told her.

Desire was having mixed emotions about everything. She felt as if though she was alone even though she had Rell and TJ she really had no immediate family. Although she was thankful for Rell, TJ, mark and Tyquan it still would have felt good to have a mother and a father to go to when she needed someone to talk to. Or even a sister she could go shopping with and have girl talk. Desire was ready to put everything behind her and for good this time.

"I thought you said you would never go back to that," Mattie said when she walked in.

Robert wiped his nose and looked at her.

"Listen here bitch, you don't worry about what I'm doing ya hear? I pay the cost to be the boss," Robert said as he bent down and snorted another line of the white powdery substance that was on the glass mirror.

Mattie was in no mood to argue she was almost at her breaking point because she had been playing this role for way too long. The only thing that kept her mind sane was knowing that this madness was going to end very soon.

"Fine, are you ready for dinner?" she asked as she headed to the kitchen.

"Yea you been gone long enough where the hell you been anyway?" Robert asked.

Mattie ignored him and continued to stir the pot of greens that was on the stove.

"Robert, I had an appointment and I told you about this days ago if you weren't killing your brain cells with that bullshit then you would have remembered," Mattie shot back.

Robert looked at Mattie as if she had lost her mind.

"WHO THE FUCK YOU THINK YOU TALKIN TO BITCH!" Robert yelled.

He staggered in the kitchen and got in Mattie's face. She made sure to stay near the hot pot of greens just in case Robert wanted to get hand happy.

"I really think you should back up every time you snort that shit you act crazy," Mattie said.

"Shut the fuck up! You don't worry about what I'm putting in ma system," Robert told her.

Mattie didn't respond she just started fixing the plates. She set the table and then took out a bottle of wine.

"Your food is on the counter," Mattie told him as she sat down and started to eat.

"Oh, so you just gone leave ma shit on the counter fuckin cunt," Robert snapped.

Mattie was getting so fed up with the name calling. She had been with Robert for years, but as time went on things got worse. She knew she should have left him when he got mixed up in Donnie's mess, but she didn't. Over the last few years her and Robert's relationship went downhill they showed outsiders exactly what they needed to see, but behind closed doors it was a different story. She only played the part she was supposed to play since her son got shot years ago. When desire came to North Carolina Robert told her that she had to act as if she didn't know anything and that she was just his wife. It hurt Mattie to be involved in such drama, but she had her own tricks up her sleeve.

"Robert, I am not your slave I am your wife, and until you realize that I am through with you and all the bullshit drama you brought to me and our marriage," Mattie said.

"You're not done until I say you're done. The shit that's been going on has gotten our blood written all over it," Robert told her.

Mattie got up and slammed her fist down on the table.

"I am through! I will not sit back and continue to let you take me down with you. I should have left you when you shot our son you piece of shit," Mattie yelled.

Robert had, had enough of Mattie and her smart remarks about his drug habits and the stuff he was involved in. Without thinking twice Robert went to the stove and grabbed the hot pot of greens and threw them on Mattie and began stomping her in her head.

"AHHHHHHHHHHHHHH!" Mattie screamed as she tried to protect her head with her hands.

There was no way that no one heard her because the scream she gave was chilling.

"I bet you will think before you speak next time bitch," Robert said as he went back into the living room and sat down and continued to feed his nose.

Mattie's screams still filled the house, but Robert was on cloud 99 and he didn't have a care in the world

*E*veryone was cleaning and loading their guns when Rell got a call. He didn't show any emotions his only response was

"I felt it."

"Yo, bro wats going on?" Mark and Tyquan asked at the same time.

"Terrence is in the hospital and he fucked up pretty bad," Rell told them.

"Damn what happened?" Mark asked.

"My dad is back," Rell responded.

Mark and Tyquan didn't need any further explanation they already knew what that meant.

"I'm surprised he's alive shit Tyshawn don't play no games. I was lucky to get out alive," said Tyquan.

Rell went into the kitchen and Desire followed.

"You seem real bothered by this," Desire said as she wrapped her arms around his waist.

"He wants me to come up there so we can talk. I mean at first, I wanted him dead, but at the end of the day karma is kickin' his ass," Rell told her.

Desire couldn't help but to agree with Rell. They always wondered if Terrence and Trina would get what was coming to them and it seemed as though they were. Even though they took Desire and Rell through hell apart of them still cared a little bit about Terrence and Trina.

"Do you want me to go with you?" she asked.

"Nah, I gotta do this one myself and finally get rid of all these past demons?" Rell told her.

"Ok, well you know I'm here if you need me," Desire said.

"I know and thank you for that bae," Rell said as he bent down to kiss.

It was finally getting dark outside and they were all preparing for the big show down.

"I can't wait to kill dis nigga," said RJ.

They were all dressed in black and ready to kill.

"Is Tyquan here with the car yet?" Rell asked.

"Yea bro just pulled up let's roll?" Mark responded.

Everyone left out and got in the car that Tyquan had stolen. The car ride to Robert's place was silent. No one talked, everyone was just lost in their thoughts. They got to Robert's place around 12:30 am. They all made sure their guns was loaded and then got out of the car. Desire said a small prayer before she got out.

Rell seen her and then grabbed her hand "Everything's gone be cool don't worry," he told her.

She nodded her head yes and followed him to Robert's house.

"On the count of three we kickin' his shit in," said RJ.

"Cool on three 1, 2, 3," Mark counted and then him and Rell kicked in the door.

"YEA MUTHAFUCKA WASSUP NOW!" Tyquan yelled as he ran in.

Robert jumped up like his ass was on fire "The fuck yawl doing breaking in ma house? Desire what's going on?" he asked.

"I should be asking you that Slim how could you, you fuckin bitch made ass nigga?" Desire asked him.

Robert staggered back and then grabbed his beer off the table.

"You always were one emotional ass bitch," said Robert as he took a swig of his beer.

WHAP! was all you heard as Rell went hard across

Robert's face with his chrome desert eagle "Don't you ever fuckin disrespect ma wife bitch nigga," Rell snapped.

Robert grabbed his bloody eye when he finally focused in on who hit him his good eye got wide.

"This is bullshit I killed you," Robert said in shock.

"No muthafucka you thought you killed me," Rell said.

He then turned to RJ and gave him a nod as if to say handle your business.

"Well, well, well it seems like you're the one caught off guard and I'm the one with the gun humph Déjà vu," said RJ.

Robert couldn't believe what he was seeing "Son you have to realize what position I was in back then," he pleaded.

"Bullshit, you shot me and you didn't give a shit if I was alive or dead. Well I survived dad and I'm here in the flesh if it wasn't for mom I wouldn't have made it," RJ explained.

Robert's facial expression turned into a deadly one. He had no clue that Mattie had known that their son was alive. For all these years Robert thought that he had killed his first and only son. To find out that Mattie knew about him being alive burned him up inside he felt betrayed.

"That stupid bitch knew you were alive," Robert spat.

RJ couldn't take the disrespect so he shot Robert twice in the leg

"Uuurgghh," Robert growled in pain.

"Talk that shit now," said RJ.

Everyone sat back and watched as the father and son went at it. They all came to have a chance at killing Robert, but the real fight was between them two. Robert looked over at desire and smiled weakly

"I'm sorry niece, but I had to do what I had to do and your father put himself in harm's way for stealing your mother from Donnie," he explained.

Desire couldn't believe he had the nerve to say something like that.

"Are you fucking serious? How dare you say that? All this because my mother loved him instead of Donnie's bitch ass? You been playing me since day one and I actually thought you cared," Desire said.

Robert started to laugh like a maniac "I didn't even give a damn about my own son shit happens and you need to get over it. It's bitches like you and your mother that makes situations like this even more fucked up than it already is," said Robert.

Those were his last words before RJ, Rell, and Desire riddled his body with bullets.

"That will be the last time you disrespect ma mother you pussy ass nigga," Desire said as she spit on him.

"Oh shit," said Tyquan. Everyone looked towards the kitchen.

"What man?" Rell asked.

"I think she dead," Tyquan said as he backed away.

RJ legs got weak as he walked in the kitchen he was hoping that this was just a dream. When he seen his mother on the floor she had blisters and burns everywhere. Her head was busted open and blood was still leaking out. He knew she was dead but he didn't want to believe it. He bent down and checked her pulse, but there was none.

"She's gone," RJ said barely above a whisper.

His heart became heavy at that very moment. His mother had been there for his since the shooting she never turned her back on him. He walked back into the living room and reloaded his gun and emptied his clip into his father.

"That was for my mother, James, Marie, Desire, Rell, and finally me rest in hell slim" said RJ.

"We gotta go," said Mark.

"Yawl go I'll take care of everything here," RJ told them.

"Man, we just can't leave you like this," Rell said.

RJ walked up to him and gave him dap.

"You and ya wife been through enough yawl go home and never looked back. Yawl helped me confront ma past demon's yawl did enough now go I'll keep in touch," said RJ.

They all wasted no time getting out of there. When they got in the car and started to pull off the house exploded into flames. Everyone jumped and looked in awe as the house went in flames they couldn't even touch bases on what just happened. People were losing their lives left and right all because of jealousy and lies. Once they made it back home Mark and Tyquan dropped Desire and Rell off so they could go get rid of the car.

ell couldn't believe he had butterflies in his stomach as he made his way to Terrence room. When he got to the door he made sure his gun was in good reach just in case Terrence wanted to get crazy.

"Iight lord I ain't came to you in a while, but right now a brotha need you," Rell said to himself.

He finally walked in and seen Terrence laying on his stomach going through his phone.

"Wassup?" Rell said once he walked in. Terrence looked over and smiled

"Wassup nigga I started to think you wasn't gone come," Terrence said as he extended his hand out.

Rell dapped him up and then sat down "So wassup you wanted to talk?" Rell said.

"Yea I'ma get straight to the point. I know shit ain't been the best between us, but I'm just tryna squash all the bullshit," Terrence told him.

Rell didn't respond right away he just stared at Terrence for a while. He put his hands in his sweat pants before he started talking.

"You took me and ma family through a lot of shit. You put ma son and ma wife's life in danger. You ain't got me fucked up you got me fucked down if you think shit gone be all peaches and cream," Rell told him.

"I understand that and I apologize. I know I'ma nasty fucked up nigga and I can admit that, but mommy had a lot to do with us beefin'. Everything I did, I did it for her; I know I'm a grown ass man and I should have ma own mind, but I'm man enough to admit that I'm fucked up in the head and we got some fucked up parents," said Terrence.

"We do, but you should've used all that negative shit and turned it into a positive instead of feeding off it in a negative way and tryna fuck everybody life up cas yours all fucked up," Rell said.

Terrence got quiet this was the first time in years since him and Rell actually talked without violence being involved.

"You right, and I should've done that but I didn't and I'm paying for that now. I'm sitting up here with a fuckin gash in ma back and on top of that I just found out I got AIDS not too long ago. I already done cut Diane off she's the reason I'm in this situation now, but I let it get this bad it's ma fault and I'm payin' for it," Terrence told him.

Rell actually felt bad for Terrence he never wanted to see anything bad happen to him, but he brought this on his self.

"I appreciate you owning up to everything, but I ain't gone beat around the bush and tell you that we gone be cool from this point on because I'd be lying but what I will say is that I forgive you for everything you've done to me and my family. I wish you the best from here on out and maybe someday we could be cool," Rell said as he got up.

That cut Terrence deep he knew that Rell wasn't going to just put everything behind him and give him another chance just like that, but he was wishful thinking.

"I can't do nothin, but respect that. Tell Desire I'm sorry for everything and that hopefully after what I done Trina will think twice about spreading that shit to anyone else," said Terrence.

Rell nodded and turned to walk out until Terrence stopped him.

"I don't know how much longer I'm a live for, but I pray and hope that I'm alive when you kill dad," said Terrence.

Rell didn't respond he just walked out. When Rell got to his car he was full of emotions, but he made sure he didn't let a tear drop. He was glad that Terrence finally admitted everything, but what made him mad was that he waited so long to do it. Rell realized that him and Terrence would never have a relationship and he was ok with that. He just hoped that Terrence would make a change for the better and never try to cross him and his family again or the next time he will be forced to kill a part of him.

"Bitch if you mess this up ya pussy won't be the only thing cut up," Tyshawn snapped at Trina as he cleaned his machete.

Trina sat on the edge of the bed in the dirty hotel loading her gun. She didn't know how Tyshawn found her, but he did and she could see why everyone was so afraid of him. He was Terrence 50 times worse and the abuse she went through in the little bit of time he had her was unbelievable. She wished she could just go to sleep and wake up from this nightmare. Diane was sucking Tyshawn's dick as he cleaned his machete. Trina had no idea why she was so shocked that Diane was acting like all of this was normal. When Tyshawn bust his nut he never moaned as Diane continued to swallow his kids he continued to clean his machete. This shit was way too real for Trina. After Diane was done she got up and lit a cigarette

"You know Terrence really disappointed me," she said as she blew out smoke.

"Well that little bitch made nigga is dead so you don't gotta worry about that bullshit no more," Tyshawn spat.

He had everyone thinking Terrence was dead, but little do he know he was wrong. When Trina heard that she felt a knot in her stomach. A part of her was happy, but then a part of her was broken. She loved Terrence, but after what he did to her she hated him. Trina felt as though it wasn't his place to do that to her. It was his fault for not using protection.

"So, when are we going to kill them?" Trina asked.

"Tonight, Robert told me everything I needed to know so we good to go," he responded and Diane smiled.

Shit Just Got Real

esire was taking a hot shower when she thought she heard gunshots. She knew the guys was outside so she thought they were probably playing around. She turned off the water and then wrapped her towel around her. As Desire was putting on her clothes she heard glass shatter and at that moment she knew something was going on so she grabbed her gun and turned off the bedroom lights. Desire slowly opened the door and crept out. She had a nervous feeling in her stomach, but she kept her cool.

"RELL!" she called out

Before Desire could take another step, she felt cold steel behind her head.

"Bitch get outside," the voice said behind her.

She remembered that voice and knew it was Diane.

"Where is Rell?" she asked.

"Don't worry about that now get outside like I said bitch and drop the gun while you're at it," Diane barked.

Desire did as she was told and dropped the gun. When she walked outside to the backyard she saw Trina holding a gun on Rell who was bleeding from the mouth and mark who was bleeding from a cut on his chest. Desire felt her body get hot when she seen Trina.

"Ahhhh Robert didn't tell me you were so beautiful, chocolate, and thick," Tyshawn said when he finally saw desire.

"Fuck you!" Desire spat.

"Watch your mouth bitch," Diane said as she hit desire with the gun.

Desire fell to the ground even though she wasn't hit that hard she played it off.

"Weak bitches fall easy," said Diane.

"You see this right here this is what's gonna happen to you Terrell. This little nigga disrespected me and he thought he was gonna get away with it," Tyshawn explained.

Diane walked over to Rell and rubbed his face and then hit him with the butt of her gun. Rell stumbled back, but didn't fall. His lip was busted and he had a bloody nose, but he was still standing. Desire lifted her head up a little and saw Tyshawn waving something back in forth in his hand as he spoke. When she got a clear view, she put her hand over her mouth to stop herself from screaming. It was Tyquan. He had Tyquan's head in his hand and his bloody machete in his other hand. Desire knew this wasn't no game Tyshawn was out to kill and wasn't going to stop until his mission was accomplished. Desire started to scoot backwards to try and get her gun from in the house. When she reached inside she felt a hand grab her.

"Shhh," he told her.

When she looked back it was Terrence. He looked terrible. Since Terrence said he could feel when Rell was in trouble and vice versa she knew that that's why he was here.

He handed her the gun "Just shoot and don't stop," he told her.

Desire was so scared that her hands couldn't stop shaking, but after seeing Tyshawn hold Tyquan's head in his hand she knew that being scared wasn't going to help her out of this situation. She counted to 3 in her head and then got up and started shooting.

Pop, pop, pop, pop, pop, pop.

She and Terrence blasted together. Desire noticed that Diane was his main target. He shot Tyshawn twice, but he kept coming. Rell ran over and tackled him and Terrence ran over and started kicking him. Mark didn't care if Trina was a girl or not he hit her with a quick right that broke her jaw instantly.

"Stupid bitch you just won't stop," said Mark.

Tyshawn was unstoppable Rell and Terrence were no match for him. After being shot twice and tackled to the ground being punched and kicked he still came back harder. Mark ran over trying to help, but Tyshawn punched him in the face and knocked him back. Terrence was trying to snap Tyshawn's neck, but he bit him

"Ahhhhh!" Terrence yelled in pain.

Rell was punching and pulling on Tyshawn so he wouldn't get to his machete. Tyshawn kicked Rell in his face and his snapped back. When desire seen that her heart dropped because she thought he was dead. When Tyshawn finally got a hold of his machete Terrence tried to get up and run, but Tyshawn grabbed him and went across his back again opening the same wound. Terrence couldn't scream that's how much pain he was in. He fell to the ground and just laid there as blood and flesh gushed out of his back. Desire closed her eyes and pulled the trigger until all she could hear was a clicking sound. She knew she had her eyes closed for a long time because when she finally opened them Rell was taking the gun out of her shaking hand.

"It's ok Des it's over now," Rell told her as he took the gun.

She looked at Tyshawn who had numerous gunshot wounds to the body including a single gunshot to the head. Rell walked over and emptied his clip into Tyshawn's body he wanted to make sure he was never coming back. Desire walked over to where Trina was laying. This was the last straw of jealousy and betrayal that Trina could ever do to her and her family.

"You will do anything to hurt me. You don't give a damn about anyone, but yourself," Desire said.

Trina tried to speak but she couldn't.

"After all these years, I tried to just move on from you and my past, but you kept coming back trying to hurt and kill me and my family. Well I'ma make sure you never harm me or my family again. It's clear that you never saw me as your sister and you showed me that you would do anything to see me fail or to see me dead. Your ma past and I'ma make sure you stay that way," Desire said as she picked up Diane's gun.

Trina's eyes got wide.

"fuck y," before Trina could get the rest of the words out Desire shot her twice in the chest and she went down.

She never thought it would ever get to this point, but Trina was no longer a sister to her. Desire had finally killed off the rest of her past, and she had no regrets in doing it. Rell took out his cell and made a call. 20 minutes later they all saw red, white, and blue lights. Desire knew this had to be the end she was going to jail for life.

3 MONTHS LATER...

*D*iane sat in her cell tracing the brick wall with her finger. It's been 3 months since the death of Tyshawn and she missed him. She ended up in hole 4 times since she been there due to her snapping on other inmates. Diane couldn't wait until she got out so she could finish Rell off once and for all. Even though she had life she still was planning on killing him. Diane was in critical condition after the shooting. She survived, but she could no longer talk. When Terrence shot her one of the bullets hit her in her neck. She went into an emergency surgery. The doctors did the best they could but she suffered from unilateral vocal cord paralysis. Diane was angry, but a little happy at the same time. She was angry because Rell and Terrence was still alive and Tyshawn was dead, and she was happy because Tyquan was dead. She felt as though she got some enjoyment out of everything. It was chow time so Diane headed out of her cell and got in line with the rest of the inmates. She was well known so no one tried her. A lot of people were afraid of Diane and made sure to steer clear of her. When she got to the cafeteria and got her food she was headed back to her table and a group of women surrounded her. It was over as soon as the second poke punctured her lung. Everyone went and sat down like nothing happened. When the guards came, no one had seen or heard anything. Diane was pronounced dead right there.

elaware New Jersey,
Desire and Rell sat on their patio looking at TJ play in the backyard. Everything seemed so right. Rell was pretty broken up after Tyquan was killed, but he knew he was in a better place. Mark had gotten a place right next door to Rell and Desire and he even was dating someone. Terrence got out of the hospital 2 months after the incident and moved to Richmond Virginia. He started helping out with the H.I.V awareness programs and started helping troubled teenage boys not go down the same path he did.

"Ok can I have my son's back now?" Desire asked Debra.

"Oh, girl you need to be resting now sit your tail down," Debra said as she shooed her away.

Rell laughed and grabbed one of the babies from Debra.

"Ight I think I got Tyrell," Rell joked.

"You better not mix up my babies," Desire told him.

After everything happened Desire went into labor she had no clue that she was pregnant, but she was and she had two beautiful twin boys. Rell named them both even though it was a shock that he was a father again and had no time to plan or set things up he was still excited. Their names were Tyrell and Tyquan Williamson he made sure Tyquan name was carried on. Desire had recently found out that the locked room from their other house was a baby room that Rell had set up for whenever they had another.

"So, how does it feel to be a father again?" Desire asked.

"It feels good I just wish Tyquan was here to see his nephews. I feel like I could have done more to protect him," Rell told her.

Desire rubbed his back.

"Baby, you did all you could. Don't ever think for one second that this was your fault. Right now, Tyquan is looking down at you smiling. He is now your guardian angel and if anyone ever tries to harm us again he will be right there to protect us," Desire said.

Rell kissed Tyrell on the forehead he had 3 sons and he planned on raised them the best way he knew how. TJ ran on the patio and tried to pick up Tyquan

"No, no, no go wash your hands boy," Debra told him as she put her hand up as a stop sign.

"Awe come on," TJ pouted.

"Awe come on my foot you better go wash your hands and make sure you put some germ ex on because you've been playing in the dirt," Debra said.

TJ ran to the bathroom and washed his hands when he came out desire gave him some germ ex.

"Now rub it in," Des told him.

"Oh, mommy it cold," said TJ.

"Debra bring him inside and we can all go in the living room" Desire said.

Debra and Rell brung the kids inside and they all went inside the living room. TJ sat on the couch and Debra gave him baby Tyquan.

"Now be careful," Debra told him.

"I got this," TJ responded and they all fell out into laughter.

"Lord I don't know what I'm going to do with 3 of you," Desire said.

"Cut it out I'm not that bad," Rell replied.

"I know baby I'm just joking," Desire said as she gave him a kiss.

"Mhm yawl better stop that's how yawl got these two," Debra said with folded arms.

Rell smiled "I need my girl now," he told her.

"Whew! I don't know how about we let the boys hit 1 then we can work on our girl," Desire said.

"I'm cool with that," Rell responded.

Later, that night Desire and Rell gave the kids a bath and put them to bed.

"So, after everything we been through was it all worth it," Rell asked.

Desire looked at her beautiful children and then thought back to everything that happened. People lost their lives and people got hurt. So many lies and secrets reached the surface, but everything taught Desire a valuable lesson. Jealousy is an ugly trait and sometimes blood ain't no thicker than water. She lost a lot in the process, but she gained so much more and now she was ready to let the past be the past and move on. She was ready to be a wonderful mother to her children and a wonderful wife to her husband. They both still resided in Delaware, but they moved to a new and better environment they had their previous house knocked down considering people were killed there. She thought she was going to prison, but come to find out RJ had given the police all the information they needed on his father, Tyshawn, Trina, Terrence, and Diane so if anything happened Desire, Rell, Mark, and Tyquan was acting in self-defense. Desire looked up at Rell and smiled

"Yes, it was all worth it what about you," she asked.

Rell had been through so much in his life. Sometimes he felt as though he was mentally damaged from what happened, but he turned all of the negative into a positive. After realizing that he couldn't control the way people turned out to be he tried to move on from his past, but it caught up to him. At times, he was afraid to let desire know the full story, but after seeing how much she loved him and how she was his ride or die he knew he could trust her with his soul. Rell didn't look at it as he'd lost his parents he looked at it as he got rid of two people who meant him or anyone else no good. He had a beautiful wife and three handsome sons and a wonderful mother and brother. Rell was ready to move forward and he wasn't going to let anything or anyone stop him. He was no longer going to let his past have a negative influence on his life.

"Hell, yea it was worth it," he responded.

"I love you Terrell."

"I love you too Desire," Rell said.

They dimmed the light in the kid's room and went to lay down. As they cuddled Desire prayed and hoped that her 3 boys weren't Terrell, Terrence, and Tyquan in the making. She wondered if TJ would be the last one standing like his father.

Silver Platter Hoe 4
Available Now

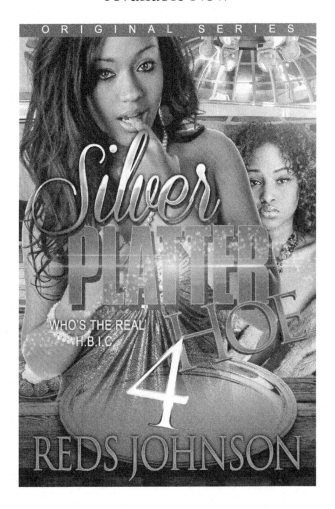

After nearly experiencing death Trina sat in her one bedroom apartment staring out the window. She couldn't believe that her own sister almost killed her. She didn't know whether she wanted revenge or whether she should just leave Desire and her family alone all together. When Trina was in the hospital nearly on life support she had time to think about a lot. She realized the beef and jealousy was all her. Trina expected Desire to fall flat on her face after she killed her parents, but she was strong and she made it through. Lost in her thoughts she didn't even realize that someone had walked into her apartment.

"Oh, shit you scared me Cash," Trina said as she jumped.

"Watchu over there thinkin' bout?" Cash asked.

Cash was Trina's boyfriend. They actually met the same day that she got out of the hospital. His whole image said *Money* and even though she wasn't capable of doing the things she used to do. That still didn't stop her from stacking her chips.

"Life baby just life and how crazy shit can get," Trina responded.

"Thinking about that bitch ass sister of yours ain't you?" Cash said as he sat down.

Trina had explained the whole situation that happened between her and Desire in her own words, but none of it was the truth. Cash was a street nigga so he thought. So ever since he and Trina got together her business was his business.

"Yea, but stuff happens," she told him.

"Nah bae I think you should get her back. Fuck that I got some bitches that would off her ass just say the word," Cash told her.

"So, you really would go after ma sister for me?" Trina asked.

"Hell yea, I mean you in no condition to do anything and since I'm ya man it's only right that I handle this situation for you," Cash boosted.

"But Desire has a boyfriend who will do anything to protect her," Trina warned.

"Fuck dat nigga. Ma name ring bells around these parts," Cash lied.

Trina smiled and that evil feeling in her heart reached the surface again. Even after Desire almost killed her she still felt like she had the upper hand because she could never be defeated. If she kept on doing what she was doing she knew that she would always be on top.

"*Trina is back,*" She thought to herself.

End of Excerpt
Get Your Copy Now!

A Letter from Reds:

To all my fans who read and enjoyed the Silver Platter Hoe series I would like to say thank you. I truly appreciate all the love and support you all showed me. To those who have asked, yes, this series is based on true events.

This series is explaining certain things I've been through. I only went through them because of another person being jealous. I wanted to show people how far jealousy can go and how lying can get you caught up in so many things. I know every family has a Trina. There might just be plenty of Desire's, and Rell's out there.

Me writing this series was a major way for me to move on from my past and forgive those who hurt me, and let them go. No matter how much criticism I got back about the title or the things that happened in this series it doesn't affect me. I lived it, I wrote it, and now I'm moving on from it. So, to all my Desire's out there don't worry trouble doesn't last forever.

Reds Johnson also known as Anne Marie, is a twenty-three-year-old independent author born and raised in New Jersey. She started writing at the age of nine years old, and ever since then, writing has been her passion. Her inspirations were Danielle Santiago, and Wahida Clark. Once she came across their books; Reds pushed to get discovered around the age of thirteen going on fourteen.

To be such a young woman, the stories she wrote hit so close to home for many. She writes urban, romance, erotica, bbw, and teen stories and each book she penned is based on true events; whether she's been through it or witnessed it. After being homeless and watching her mother struggle for many years, Reds knew that it was time to strive harder. Her passion seeped through her pores so she knew that it was only a matter of time before someone gave her a chance.

Leaping head first into the industry and making more than a few mistakes; Reds now has the ability to take control of her writing career. She is on a new path to success and is aiming for bigger and better opportunities.

Visit my website www.iamredsjohnson.com

MORE TITLES BY REDS JOHNSON

SILVER PLATTER HOE 6 BOOK SERIES

HARMONY & CHAOS 6 BOOK SERIES

MORE TITLES BY REDS JOHNSON

NEVER TRUST A RATCHET BITCH 3 BOOK SERIES

TEEN BOOKS

A PROSTITUTE'S CONFESSIONS SERIES

CLOSED LEGS DON'T GET FED SERIES

MORE TITLES BY REDS JOHNSON

OTHER TITLES BY REDS JOHNSON

Made in the USA
Monee, IL
14 August 2020